Yes, You Are Home

A novel presented in memoir and film

William M. Trently

iUniverse LLC
Bloomington

YES, YOU ARE HOME
A novel presented in memoir and film

iUniverse books may be ordered through booksellers or by contacting:

iUniverse LLC
1663 Liberty Drive
Bloomington, IN 47403
www.iuniverse.com
1-800-Authors (1-800-288-4677)

ISBN: 978-1-4917-3367-7 (sc)
ISBN: 978-1-4917-3368-4 (e)

Library of Congress Control Number: 2014908112

Printed in the United States of America.

iUniverse rev. date: 05/06/2014

Contents

ACKNOWLEDGEMENTS

Thank you to Bertha Trently, Stephen Mertz, David Trently, and Devin Trently. Thank you to The Teaching Company for giving us all the golden gift of knowledge; among their outstanding professors are the following who figured greatly in this book: David Christian, Stuart Sutherland, Brian Fagan, Peter N. Stearns, Barbara J. King, Neil deGrasse Tyson, and Robert Greenberg. Essential references: *Prehistoric Life* (Dorling Kindersley, 2009), *Earth—The Ever-Changing Planet* (Donald Silver, Ph.D., 1989, Random House), *Maps of Time— An Introduction to Big History* (David Christian, 2004, University of California Press), *Nine Alive!* (stories and photos from the Associated Press, 2002, SP L.L.C.), and *All Nine Alive!* (from the pages of the Pittsburgh Post-Gazette, 2002, Triumph Books).

To everybody, of course.

BREAKING NEWS: Scientists at the Nationale Institute of Research have discovered an eyewitness's memoir and actual film footage of the creation of Earth and its subsequent history up to the present day. The data was extracted from as-of-yet unnamed microscopic cellular structures. This serendipitous find may provide answers to some of the most baffling questions that inhabitants of this planet have encountered over the centuries.

ONE

It was and is a harsh, rugged, precarious and often unforgiving landscape, incessantly rearranged by asteroids, earthquakes, winds, and rains, its underbelly a wriggling subterranean cauldron of bending, melting, shifting rocks, constructed over a vast span of time in a huge area of space from tiny particles of gas and dust, a fragile home into which all the little lives that have come and gone were invited to happen, filled with an abundance of pain, cruelty, and misery, and beauty and love and kindness.

*

A long time before today, a star, maybe more than one, collapsed and died, blowing apart into countless pieces which formed a vast cloud of atoms, cold gas, and dust that occupied an area several times larger than the present solar system. This enormous, valuable junkyard of elemental debris slowly drifted through space as one gigantic mass, as if it were a pollen cloud remaining mostly intact without significant dissipation. When viewed in its totality, I could discern a floating menagerie of something that was different from the clear, empty void surrounding it, like a hazy amorphous veil standing in stark contrast against the dark vacant background of the universe.

In some places the air had the appearance of wavy irregularity as when a tank is filled with gas at the pump or when heat radiates from a sun-scorched asphalt road in the middle of summer. Much of what I could observe depended upon the angle of light beaming from the space car's headlights, brought out even more vividly when using the enhanced sensor technology. It was interesting and fascinating. Other nooks in this neighborhood of the cosmos sometimes issued as if in the guise of a billowy accumulation of dust extricated from an upright vacuum cleaner bag. Just looking at this particular visual presentation threatened to incite a sneeze attack, and I was grateful to be enclosed within the protected confines of the space car!

The interplay of these stray unorganized elements was naturally affected right from the start by the physical laws of the universe. As atoms and molecules bumped into each other, sometimes they bounced back apart with a quick hello and goodbye, but at other times they preferred to socialize at length, remaining physically joined in either a somewhat casual or often more intimate embrace. When, eventually, a cluster of these latter pieces became larger through further collisions, the gravitational pull exerted by this group upon other floating particulates in the vicinity grew more forceful. In this way, more and more atoms and molecules could be lured in, brought together into microscopic, irregularly-shaped, relatively loosely-assembled groupings of dust. It was a handful of wet snow patted timidly against another, becoming a larger mass of slush, not yet molded into a hard round snowball.

Nonetheless, over time, the individual particles mingling in most of these groups became compressed tighter together, forming hard, denser clumps. The snowball was now being compacted. And as additional molecules joined these and they grew slowly in size, eventually they went beyond dust, becoming small, hard pebbles of different shapes. The exterior shell of the space car that I piloted was introduced to these when the pebbles collided with it and inflicted shallow dints. These did not, fortunately, compromise the structural integrity of the vehicle, although they did alter the once-smooth surface so that it now took on the texture of something resembling an orange peel.

Over the course of many more years, the pebbles would ever-so-slowly grow to become big rocks. The larger of these now presented more of a threat to my vehicle and so I had to navigate carefully away from any heavily-populated rock fields. Eventually many of these conglomerations, floating so quietly in space, grew to be hundreds of meters in length and width and then continued to expand at the sluggish rate of perhaps a few centimeters more per year over the course of the next million years.

The first of these monster rocks I saw was frightening, jumping out at me from the darkness of space like an ominous shark descried suddenly without warning by a scuba diver. Its asymmetric shape was long and unbalanced, slender at one end but fat at the opposite, definitely not spherical. Subsequent to that first dread-inducing sighting, I would come to see hundreds more of these space boulders every few hours, all of dissimilar shapes and sizes.

Thus over the long stretch of time, what had begun as small pebbly assemblages had now become so much more massive, akin to something my kids would have called "dinosaur boulders." Astounding, when you think of the infinitesimal particles from which they grew. But, after all, from what but a tiny seed does the thickest tree begin. Given enough occasions and favorable conditions, small things can certainly grow into herculean structures.

In time, the far-reaching, fat cloud of gas and dust, small particulates, and rocks of all sizes slowly—very slowly—rotated en masse, unhurriedly, around a central axis—a slow-motion carousel, a repressed pinwheel. To view its movement in real time from space was reminiscent of watching an hour hand on a clock move almost imperceptibly through its circuitous rounds.

Then, about four-and-a-half billion years ago, the spinning speed velocity increased. I was no longer watching an hour hand, which had now been abandoned in favor of, firstly, a step-up to the pace of the minute hand and later to that of the hand marking the passing of seconds. The mass of many materials was moving increasingly faster.

As nature's laws continued to exert their omniscient forces, the bulbous cloudy configuration began to contract and flatten, forming the shape of a very clearly recognizable disc. Once the swirling mass had assumed the conformation of a disk, I felt coerced to discard the entire timepiece analogy in describing its velocity. To me, it now appeared as a beefed-up phonograph record playing at its slowest speed setting. It moved like this for a very long while, but then over the course of a further elapse of ages gradually picked up a considerable degree of additional swiftness. The DJ changed the tempo from thirty-three to forty-five rpm. This took a long time to develop, but I had all the time in the world to watch.

Within the spinning disk, the heaviest materials tended to move toward the center, which took on a bulging, more spherical shape—like a golf ball had appeared in the center of the phonograph record. Here, the laws of chemistry produced extreme heat and luminosity as hydrogen was converted into helium by the process of nuclear fusion. This intumescence at the middle of the giant swirl was destined to become a new star, the sun. Just like everything else so far, this took a long time to happen—in this case, millions of years. The sun's temperature at its center would become as hot as fifteen-million degrees and there was enough fuel inside this star to keep it burning for about eight-to-ten-billion years. Thus it warmed the cosmos in its immediate vicinity. Indeed, I was glad about that since it was a welcome change to the coldness of space.

I remember telling each of my three children after they graduated from college that when you are enclosed within your car driving to work in the morning, do not ever forget that the world is around you. Always keep in mind, I tried to instill in them, that it is important to avoid becoming trapped within a narrow, uninformed, and confined view that is aloof from the totality of existence that surrounds you, a snare easy to fall into as you navigate the daily routine's mundane trivialities. The world is around you, but you are in your car. At least roll down the window, I instructed! Take in the bigger picture, I said, and your place within it. When you are greeted by the intense glaring sun over the asphalt road that rolls out ahead of you, and you squint to be able to see, and you reach for your sunglasses and feel the warmth on your face and hands, remember how this awe-inspiring structure, a star, originated.

Away from this centrally-positioned spherical protosun, the disk was less dense, more diffuse. As the gigantic phonograph record spun even faster and the floating junkyard of stuff got whipped around, picking up even more momentum, several orbits were laid down, each a superhighway on which icy gas and dust and rock were to travel, over and over again, around the sun in roughly the same plane while following a regular, predictable timetable.

The molecules, gas, ice, and rocks in each orbit traveled together. I selected a particular orbit and rode alongside the massive rocks. I galloped through a levitated field of boulders—a spectacular obstacle course laid out as if all of the sprawling Boulder Field in Pennsylvania was multiplied a thousand-fold and then magically hoisted up into the air as airborne suspended rubble, stretching through space in a seemingly endless parade. Or, if you can relate more to the rugged New England coast, imagine those lengthy fields of boulders at the water's edge at low tide hoisted into the corridors of the atmosphere. The sheer massiveness of it—it seemed everywhere I looked were space boulders—made me pause in awe, but not for too long since I had to constantly reroute the Space Nomad (the name we had given to the space car) so as not to crash or be struck by my fellow, inanimate and petrified orbital travel companions. I needed to keep a hand on the rudder and an eye on the road ahead and to the sides and behind as I dodged these floating monoliths, many of which would eventually crash into and join with other structures.

Most of the time I simply navigated a safe distance away from the main street of the orbit and could thereby successfully avoid collisions. But there were times when the fighter jet pilot in me came out and I intentionally flew my aircraft into the congested road of debris. It was fun flying at full speed, dodging all the objects and performing acrobatic maneuvers where I would turn my direction at the drop of a dime. A jink to the right would more often than not be followed by an evasive tumbling somersault in a completely opposite vector. A little crazy and risky, perhaps, but who else do you think gets selected to command these kinds of space missions in the first place?

Attracting the most material from the surroundings, the largest bodies formed loosely-bound, irregularly-shaped masses of various sizes and odd shapes. Many of them looked like an assortment of boulders glued together in peculiar three-dimensional arrangements, with a lumpy, bumpy surface all around like the skin of a toad or the ripped, muscular body of that orange superhero, The Thing.

I took pictures of these colorful sundry concoctions and affectionately gave names to many of them. After all, they hung around for thousands of years so of course I became quite familiar with them. I knew each very well, in the same way that you can identify the moon or constellations in your nighttime sky. I even made several of the photos into glossy postcards. One that I called "Irwin" looked like a moon-sized basketball with large bumps and odd-shaped protuberances jutting out to the front and sides on the perimeter. The problem, however, was that I had no postage stamps to affix to my postcards. Heck, I had no mail carriers, either, to deliver these to anybody. So they just sat on my desk for a few generations before I ultimately was forced to relocate them, sadly, to the bottom of a cardboard box I stashed in the basement level of the space car.

In time, some of these mega-clumps became spherical and big enough and organized sufficiently to be classified as planets, one being the earth. The other rock groupings remained as planetesimals, asteroids, comets, meteoroids, or other assorted smaller entities.

As conglomerations increased in size to become planets, their gravitational pull commensurately increased and they continued to draw in heavy rock structures from their immediate surroundings with a most ferocious force, giving rise to a period of intense bombardment. Earth would experience this for perhaps a billion years. A space boulder thirty meters in diameter could hit the earth at a speed of forty-five thousand miles per hour, striking with a force equivalent to two megatons of TNT, about one-hundred atom bombs' worth of energy. The surface topography of the assaulted celestial body would be incessantly rearranged by these violent crashes. On the one hand, this facilitated further growth, as more mass was fused to the large body. But sometimes, particularly powerful crashes could break off a significant chunk of the planet, sending it away, off into orbit around the same torso from which it had once been affixed, becoming a moon or a stray orphan asteroid or meteoroid. Indeed, Earth's moon was founded in this way.

One day during this intense bombardment, I landed my space car on the surface of Earth. The steam and hot gases like methane, nitrogen, and ammonia from inside the earth had been escaping through volcanoes to join the abundant hydrogen and helium in the air to form the first atmosphere around this planet. There was very little oxygen. Due to this particular mix of chemicals, the sky was red, not blue. The outdoor temperature was dangerously and oppressively hot. Sporadic drawn-out hissing produced by gas expelled from the deeper voids within the ground emerged to my right at one moment, only to be negated in the next instant and transferred to the left, followed by a repeat of the pattern, effectively surrounding me in a stereophonic ambience. It was like someone was preparing numerous demitasses of espresso in a café for giants. This was the appropriately-named Hadean Epoch, for it was indeed a hell on Earth. Fortunately I had Oxygen Bubble technology which enabled me to breathe and live in this foreign environment without having to be chained to a cumbersome facemask and tank like in the old days.

From the ground surface of Earth, looking across the horizon into the sunset, I saw that the sky was practically littered with rocky celestial bodies of various sizes orbiting the planet. The largest structures hovering in the firmament looked like moons, with the sun reflecting off them to create shadows so that they were presented in various phases to my line of vision. What a sight it was to see at least twenty of these huge imposing globes of stone suspended and scattered throughout the evening sky, knowing that eventually many of those would be

William M. Trently

drawn in by gravity and would crash into Earth's surface, greatly altering the topography with each incident.

It was a miracle I was not injured or squashed by the aerial bombings while I played my violin. It was atop a high elevation that I sat, garbed in tee shirt and khaki shorts, upon a makeshift granite chair, in a place that fortunately remained relatively stable, for the moment, despite periodic earthquakes rumbling throughout the day. I kept my docksiders on my feet in case there would be a need to suddenly run and relocate. My cat sat and listened as I played. The space car was parked off to the side. I sweated profusely because of the high temperatures. The entire terrain on Earth was completely rocky, painted in the colors of rocks, with predominant shades of gray, brown, and black, with a noticeable absence of any plants or water bodies whatsoever at this time. We occupied a wide ledge at the promontory of the highest mountain around, offering a three-hundred sixty degree view where we could see at least ten active volcanoes as well as several other non-volcanic mountains that presented imposingly jagged, pointy, sharp-angled, asymmetric silhouettes against the backdrop of the horizon. We stayed far enough away from the edge of the cliff so to avoid taking an accidental slide down. The cat and I were the only living things around that could actually be seen with the naked eye. It was amazing we were able to stay alive here. This infant planet was a dangerous, precarious place upon which to live. It was difficult trying to perform one of my favorite violin sonatas, a piece much like Vivaldi's *Four Seasons,* when the ground began shaking violently; indeed, I hit many wrong notes while the earth trembled.

As the bombardment continued at the surface of Earth, the interior of the planet formed. It was at the center of this planet where the heaviest rocks made of iron migrated, about four-thousand miles down to the center of the sphere. Here they became compressed tightly together to create a densely-packed solid iron inner core. This place was under incredible pressure and became nearly as hot as the sun. Surrounding the inner core was an outer core of red-hot molten metal like a tremendously huge vat of glowing liquefied metal roiling and splashing about in the heart of a Pittsburgh steel mill. Just picturing this made me feel the hard sweat-drenched drudgery followed by anticipation of freedom a steelworker would get upon hearing the whistle blow to mark the end of the work shift so he could head out with his buddies to drink an Iron City lager at the corner bar! The entire core with its inner and outer layers was larger than the planet Mars, so this was a really big factory.

Surrounding the core was a mantle layer that was also under high pressure. It was made up of rock that was sometimes solid but which at other times flowed as a molten liquid called magma. It was as if it were alive, constantly changing and writhing, in a state of flux. What a dynamic, tempestuous environment that waged its violent thermal wars beneath our feet!

A thin crust made up the final layer of the earth. On top of the mantle, this crust of rocks was anywhere from three to fifty-six miles thick. If the earth was an apple, the crust would be the thickness of the fruit's skin. This outer lamina of the planet was cooler than the intensely heated deeper layers.

Deep under the surface you would hear the grinding and grating noises created as large slabs of rock rubbed against each other. Occasionally their positions shifted drastically and some rocks would be pushed down under others. Sometimes, if the pressure became so great, the bars of metal would snap and cause a hideous roar while the reverberations shot to the surface of the planet, earthquakes and tremors riddling through the epidermis.

The rocks beneath the surface that were in the form of molten magma flowed like slow-moving boiling rivers in places. And as magma and its hot gases oozed into dead-end nooks and alleyways of solidified and seemingly stable rock configurations, sometimes the arrangement would collapse from the intense pressure without a moment's warning and disruptions to the integrity of the crustal surface could occur. I often worried that some small change deep within the mantle might transpire which could set off a chain reaction of other cataclysmic alterations, perhaps leading to a structural disintegration at the surface where I was parked.

Indeed, one time the subterranean world shifted so much that an enormous slab of stone was pushed up from a mile below the crust, piercing through the surface to form a new mountain and valley. In this process of subduction, a plate of solid igneous rock was in turn displaced, diving underneath the invading leviathan, sucked down into the depths of the mantle's magma. Once there, much of that slab melted when it became hot enough. Then, at a later time, that same molten mass would flow out of a volcano and become lava which would eventually cool to form new rocks.

This rock cycle was fascinating. When a person looks at a rock today, and maybe even touches it if it is close by, it would not be ridiculous for him or her to wonder where the stone had been in its travels. Oh, if it could just talk! Would it explain how it was actually once a tree destined to become sedimentary rock, a broad-leafed tree that a baby stegosaurus brushed up against while using the foliage for shelter as it sought to hide from a potential antagonist? Would it tell a tale of having been to the center of the earth, or close enough, once or twice in four billion years? Is it now made up of many different individual parts of rocks that came from places very remote from each other? And would this rock say it hates where it most recently ended up, bashful to be the most prominent boulder lying along the coast, projecting up above the splashing littoral waves, looking like a whale's head, covered by water at high tide, tired of tourists pointing at it during low tide? Or would that be okay with this rock—this traveler who unfortunately cannot talk to tell us?

Thus, this earth was a big rock collection packaged together in the shape of a giant ball, an assembly of assorted rocks, some hard, some molten, all in an eternal state of fluctuation. Even to the present day, this hodgepodge, this fruitcake, never stops changing. All the rocks are moving, shifting, rubbing, breaking, melting, and rearranging incessantly. They are migrating and metamorphosing, all the little movements adding up to macro alterations such as the drifting of grandiose continents into entirely new conformations and different positions over time.

One afternoon as I stood on that mountain peak where I played the violin, I heard a loud, rumbling noise as the ground shook. A large crack opened in the surface of the earth. I had a good view. I looked down into the distance from this high vantage point. The wind howled furiously and I heard steam whispering all around me. Smoke and hot gas began spewing out furiously from the menacing crack. I'll never forget the acrid smell.

That night, red-hot glowing rocks, gases, and lava shot out of the crack like fireworks at a down-home boisterous civic celebration. The dark sky was illuminated with these projectiles. Some of the tiny lava droplets were in the form of volcanic dust, while the larger ones were blasted upward as powdery ash and cinders. Millions of tons of this debris would be expelled from the earth before it all stopped for the night. These rocks and ash landed in a pile around the crack, building up to form a cone greater than one-hundred twenty feet high astonishingly by the next afternoon.

This volcanic eruption continued for weeks. The ash caused the daytime sky to be dark. It covered the ground like snow for almost as far as I could see from the mountain. Then one day lava began pouring out from the top of the volcano while a smaller amount oozed from the structure's side. Sometimes the lava shot straight up high in the air like a fountain of fire. The hot lava heated everything in its path as it flowed more than a mile away. The rocky landscape around me was transformed into a charred grey wasteland covered by ash and embers.

In time, the volcano was almost one-thousand feet tall and the river of lava had traveled five miles in all directions. Eventually the lava cooled to form mineral crystals which hardened into igneous rocks. Some that cooled more quickly became glassy black obsidian, while others formed basalt. Deep inside the earth, there were huge magma flows that, stopping short of being expelled into the earth's exterior, slowly cooled to form batholiths of granite and gabbro.

I only stayed a few months on the surface before jettisoning out of there so I could hover near but far enough away for safety, in anticipation of a potential future landing only when conditions might improve. My calculations indicated that Earth seemed to have the greatest potential to sustain life, so that is why I steered and remained near, waiting and hoping that my guesses were correct and things would settle down on the planet, which was currently permeated with an excessive degree of violent and dramatic volatility.

Life inside the space car was fairly comfortable. There were eight rooms that included a kitchen, dining area, living room, bedroom, bath, laboratory, office, and a large basement with a small gym. Oh, and there even was an attic—a good place to store things and, no, it did not have bats flying around. I kept a kayak up there and boxes of memorabilia. The space car was really like a small house of about three-thousand square feet in area. Sometimes I thought of this domicile as a sports utility vehicle with a monster jet engine that allowed it to fly, and to fly hard and ferociously.

My feline friend had jet black hair just like mine. She had splotches of snowy white fur decorating her fluffy, long-haired coat. She had her own little space aboard the homey vessel, a small nook that included her litter box, litter locker, drinking fountain with running water, and play area. In addition, she, like me, had many favorite hangouts throughout the spacecraft, each selected to suit her particular mood.

I read a great many books; travelling on a space mission such as the one I was embarked upon was certainly a great way to catch up on reading to-do lists. Actually, since I eventually ran out of new books to read, I ended up rereading multiple times the ones I had already been through. The humorous ones were most appreciated as the days turned into years, which turned into centuries and then millennia.

In addition, there was a nice film collection inside the spacecraft. A large, comfortable projection area made the screening of these movies quite enjoyable. I revisited many of these films on several occasions over the centuries, but wondered why I had even bothered in the first place to bring along some of the other, poorer quality productions on this long road trip.

I also kept in pretty good shape by regularly using the gym. My goal was always to maintain muscle tone, not to build bulk. And of course, it was essential to keep up cardiovascular health. I must admit, however, there were many occasions on which I fabricated excuses to try to dodge my scheduled workouts for sheer laziness on my part. Instead, I would just gaze out the many windows found around the ship or find something else to occupy my attention. Just like the cat, I had my preferred portholes to look through at different times of the day.

By four billion years ago the earth cooled enough to permit water molecules—two hydrogen atoms connected to one oxygen—to condense as clouds of water vapor. At that moment, when there were still no actual bodies of water to be found on the planet, I made a second landing upon the crust of the earth in anticipation of when actual precipitation would begin to descend. My calculations predicted this could happen soon. As I waited for some form of precipitate to emerge, I encountered a modest improvement in conditions on the planet's surface—though still not perfect—and so was able to stay much longer than was possible during the last time I touched down.

I will never forget that first rain, initially announcing itself to me when it began quietly knocking on the roof above my bedroom, awakening me from a deep sleep in which I was for some unknown reason dreaming vividly of teddy bears and old acquaintances having a tea party at some oceanside resort along the fringes of an arid desert.

I opened my eyes and thought, "What the . . . what was that all about?" and then realized what was going on outdoors. I ran outside, wanting so badly to get wet. I caught raindrops with my tongue, my head tilted back far, my arms outstretched upward as I laughed with joy. They descended slowly at first. I watched as individual drops landed upon the dirt of the ground, turning the color darker in the place of impact. One by one, more soil was moistened, and I began smelling the dampness. Then the precipitation became a drizzle and I will never forget the sounds it made as it became more intense. It felt good to get wet. I had waited a long time for this.

Of course I would also have to wait even longer to be able to swim anywhere, because no lakes, rivers, or oceans would be established for a very long time, not until enough rain fell to the ground to fill the lower-lying depressions so that durable reservoirs of water were created. I was like a disappointed child waiting anxiously for the bathtub to fill while only slowly-forming drops of water dripped lazily from the faucet.

I stuck around for a while, basking in the pleasure of watching the rain go on and on. But then, because the intense bombardment of the surface of Earth by circling celestial bodies became more vigorous again, I was forced to blast off into orbit where it was much safer overall, unfortunately before any rivers or lakes could materialize.

Nevertheless, after many years more of patient waiting, as I flew around the earth from high above I began to see waterways added to the landscape of mountains and valleys and volcanoes. The planet now had blue incorporated into the previously earth-tone-only palette. In modern times it would be dubbed the "water planet," with this substance covering seventy-one percent of its surface. In addition, the atmosphere had turned blue, too, as its chemical makeup changed as well. Earth had become very blue.

The intense bombardment of Earth lasted until about three-and-a-half billion years ago. After then, even continuing up to the present day, asteroids and other space rocks would still crash into the earth's surface, but not as often. And much of the remaining gas and unaccreted material in the solar system disk was eventually blown away by radiation from the sun's nuclear fusion factory, so there would be less potential villains out and about to wreak havoc.

With the relatively significant improvement in conditions, I was finally able to land permanently, my third landing, and make Earth my home, now a somewhat safer place. As a bonus, the temperature became temperate, which made things much more comfortable as well. That is, I emphasize, for the time being. The planet would go through incessant climate changes in the times ahead, as I was to come to know oh so well.

I went mountain biking over the rocky terrain. I paddled my kayak along the rivers and ocean shorelines. I hiked up and down the mountains. I skipped flat, smooth rocks across the glassy surface of wide, placid rivers. I nudged boulders from steep hillsides so I could watch them tumble and roll to the rocky floor below. When the climate became frigid I ice-skated and skied and watched snowflakes fall from the sky. It was a road trip of amazing wonder. I felt like a child every day discovering and enjoying the planet's physical features.

And so it was atop this crust where I took up residence. I sat on the roof of this warehouse of gold, uranium, diamonds, copper, iron, and other assorted rocks and minerals. Here was fairly solid ground on which to walk, for most of the time, anyway. Here was where I could live, despite the fact that under and above the ground lurked perils that could rush from hiding at a moment's notice. An otherwise good day could be ruined in an instant by any one of many bad things. Terra firma! Whoever gave it that name? It was all relative, apparently.

In addition to the less common aerial bombardments and subterranean reshuffling of rock and magma, there were the powerful forces of weathering that pestered the land. As I became familiar with the deep canyons and towering mountain peaks, the spacious flat plains, the hot deserts, and the raging shorelines, I also encountered the things that happened when the land was exposed continually to the elements of Mother Nature. There were cliff-ridden rocky shores that were incessantly being worn down by crashing ocean waves, and rivers slicing and eroding their way through the continents, and glaciers cutting patterns into the rock and dirt. There were waterfalls and rapids slowly altering the terrain. Water, the universal solvent, slowly dissolved minerals and eroded rocks into smaller particles, helping to form soil. Water made alterations to the earth's surface when it flooded low-lying areas or carried dirt and rock downstream. Water formed underground caves as it trickled through the ground. Magma could heat water under the ground so that it would be propelled upward as hot geysers. In addition to what water was capable of doing, there were the forces of wind which sandblasted rock surfaces, rounding and smoothing them and sculpturing odd-shaped formations into them such as tall narrow stone columns or perfectly round boulders appearing by themselves in the middle of the desert. The wind had the power to carry away small particles of silt and clay, sometimes for miles away. Wind could knock things over. And there also were plenty of chemical reactions going on which could degrade and alter rocks.

The agents of weathering were all around. These forces of nature most of the time worked slowly and quietly, not so dramatically. They were constantly at work, repetitive, and often barely perceptible, with periodic variations thrown in. If you would take the time to observe a single drop of water slowly creeping like an amoeba down a gentle slope of a granite rock surface, you would see some of its molecules being lost to evaporation, the rest inching their way down to a lower level. Eventually the droplet rolls into a thin crevice in the rock, where it remains and sits, to freeze on a subzero cold day. As its mass expands, it exerts stress upon the walls of the rock structure, but then releases this force when the next day the ice melts. If this happens again and again over years of time, eventually the rock can flex enough that it cleaves apart, in time breaking from the larger body.

Things changed all the time in this slow way. Because I lived for so long on this young planet, even though these miniscule processes continually played out around me almost imperceptibly, my senses became heightened and I was able to vividly see more lucidly and appreciate the micro-alterations that occurred over these elongated stretches of time. My mind became adept at perceiving, as if utilizing its own time-lapse photography over several millions of years, the macro end results that were very different from what was there to begin with. Did you ever know a field so well after having traipsed through it often one summer, only to return to it the next year to discover a terrain now unrecognizable due to different species of vegetation that had taken over? And that occurred in just one annum. Imagine the alterations you would be greeted with if you returned in a thousand years. In fact, where you are sitting today—what did it look like a hundred years ago? How about a thousand? Or a million? Was it covered by water at one time? Was there a volcano there?

These huge spans of time are truly an elusive reality for anyone to grasp fully. It is mind-boggling to absorb and comprehend such grandiose and protracted stretches of time. It could never be a simple task to attempt to get a handle on the sheer enormity of these wide open spaces of time. Think of everything that happened in the one-thousand years between 1000 CE (formerly designated "AD," or Anno Domini) and 2000 CE. There were Crusades, Dark Ages, Medieval castles, Christopher Columbus, the French Revolution, two World Wars, and the landing of humans on the moon. This was one-thousand years—a millennium. If you take one thousand of these one-thousand-year periods, you would have a million years. A million years! That's a lot of years. Now, if you went even further and took one-thousand of those one-million-year segments, you would then have a billion years!

And although most of the time all seemed quiet as these barely-perceptible pressures constantly were at work, those same forces could also at times be fast and furious, instantly recognizable as something powerful and dramatic, as during nature's periodic displays of its more intense capabilities such as when events like hurricanes, tsunamis, floods, hailstorms, tornadoes, as well as earthquakes and volcanic eruptions, took place.

The uninhabited early Earth was the training ground of storms of violence as they ripped things apart in preparation for the killing and destruction they would hand out a long time in the future when humans and animals and plants would feel the full extent of their wrath. Humans would find themselves trapped as victims of the destructive extremes of natural forces, caught up in disasters such as the floods in China in 1931 that killed at least a million people; or the tsunami in the Indian Ocean that hit Indonesia and adjacent lands in December of 2004, taking the lives of up to 310,000 people; or the earthquake in 1976 in China that killed more than 242,419 people; or the avalanche in Austria in 1954 that caused fifty-seven to perish; or the rock ice slide in Russia in 2002 that killed one-hundred twenty-five people; or the blizzard in northeastern United States in 1978 that killed one-hundred; or the blizzard in Iran in 1972 that caused four-thousand to perish; or a cyclone in Bangladesh in 1991 that killed 138,866 people. They lost all kinds of mementos, heirlooms, and treasured gifts in these disastrous events. They saw photos burn in fires and cherished letters destroyed in flood waters. Heat waves killed 70,000 in 2003 in Europe and 56,000 in Russia in 2010. In 1856 in Greece a lightning strike caused an explosion at the Palace of the Grand Masters, killing 4000. A limnic eruption took the lives of 1,744 human beings around Lake Nyos in Cameroon in 1986. Tornadoes killed 695 in the United States in 1925, 23,000 in Colombia in 1985, and 5,115 in Indonesia in 1919. And the Black Saturday brushfires of 2009 killed 173 people in Australia. And if that's not enough, on the average, every one-hundred years Earth gets hit by a particularly large asteroid that causes significant destruction. In 1908 in Siberia, a sixty-meter diameter asteroid felled 1000 square miles of forest and vaporized 100 square miles of vegetation. No crater was found because it probably exploded in midair.

So the universe may have begun about thirteen billion years ago. For my own part, I travelled through space and arrived in one particular niche of this universe, an address which happened to be that cloud of dust and gas which I earlier described, six billion years ago. Then the sun formed five billion years ago. The earth entered the scene four-and-a-half billion years ago and the period of intense bombardment began shortly after. At four billion years ago, water began to fill the low-lying depressions in the terrain. At three-and-a-half billion years ago, the intense bombardment essentially ended. These things played out mostly in slow motion, repetitively, over the vastness of time and space, with periods of intense and dramatic alterations and occasional variations.

Erupting. Evaporating. Annealing. Adhering. Bending. Denting. Growing. Evolving. Hurling. Integrating. Jolting. Flaring. Melting. Melding. Decaying. Exploding. Shoving. Separating. Tripping. Vibrating. Weathering. Opening. Plying. Pushing. Pulling. Ripping. Pinching. Oozing. Rotting. Slicing. Sanding. Scraping. Abutting. Crystallizing. Fusing. Holding. Joining. Multiplying. Accreting. Bridging. Caulking. Fissuring. Hitting. Windblasting. Torquing. Wedging. Wrinkling. Splintering. Rubbing. Affixing. Banding. Combining. Cracking. Chipping. Damaging. Decomposing. Building. Spinning. Repelling. Attracting. Banging. Freezing. Warming. Aligning. Breaking. Collapsing. Flowing. Snowing. Rotating. Sliding. Radiating. Shooting. Settling. Applying. Arranging. Fragmenting. Splitting. Braiding. Attenuating. Burning. Flaking. Crumbling. Avalanching. Buttressing. Fracturing. Bouncing. Furrowing. Millions of years pass.

Erupting. Evaporating. Annealing. Adhering. Bending. Denting. Growing. Evolving. Hurling. Integrating. Jolting. Flaring. Melting. Melding. Decaying. Exploding. Shoving. Separating. Tripping. Vibrating. Weathering. Opening. Plying. Pushing. Pulling. Ripping. Pinching. Oozing. Rotting. Slicing. Sanding. Scraping. Abutting. Crystallizing. Fusing. Holding. Joining. Multiplying. Accreting. Bridging. Caulking. Fissuring. Hitting. Windblasting. Torquing. Wedging. Wrinkling. Splintering. Rubbing. Affixing. Banding. Combining. Cracking. Chipping. Damaging. Decomposing. Building. Spinning. Repelling. Attracting. Banging. Freezing. Warming. Aligning. Breaking. Collapsing. Flowing. Snowing. Rotating. Sliding. Radiating. Shooting. Settling. Applying. Arranging. Fragmenting. Splitting. Braiding. Attenuating. Burning. Flaking. Crumbling. Avalanching. Buttressing. Fracturing. Bouncing. Furrowing. A million more years pass.

Mostly in slow motion, over the vastness of time. Plenty of repetition, but with periodic variations on the main theme. Erupting. Evaporating. Annealing. Adhering. Bending. Crunching. Plummeting. Denting. Growing. Evolving. Hurling. Integrating. Jolting. Flaring. Melting. Melding. Decaying. Exploding. Shoving. Separating. Tripping. Vibrating. Weathering. Opening. Plying. Pushing. Pulling. Ripping. Pinching. Oozing. Rotting.

Slicing. Sanding. Scraping. Abutting. Crystallizing. Fusing. Holding. Joining. Multiplying. Accreting. Bridging. Caulking. Fissuring. Hitting. Windblasting. Torquing. Wedging. Wrinkling. Splintering. Rubbing. Affixing. Banding. Combining. Cracking. Chipping. Damaging. Decomposing. Building. Spinning. Repelling. Attracting. Banging. Freezing. Warming. Aligning. Breaking. Collapsing. Flowing. Snowing. Rotating. Sliding. Radiating. Shooting. Settling. Applying. Arranging. Fragmenting. Splitting. Braiding. Attenuating. Burning. Flaking. Crumbling. Avalanching. Buttressing. Fracturing. Bouncing. Furrowing. Drip, drip, drip.

Erupting. Evaporating. Annealing. Adhering. Bending. Dropping. Plunging. Denting. Growing. Evolving. Hurling. Integrating. Jolting. Flaring. Melting. Melding. Decaying. Exploding. Shoving. Separating. Tripping. Vibrating. Weathering. Opening. Plying. Pushing. Pulling. Ripping. Pinching. Oozing. Rotting. Slicing. Sanding. Scraping. Abutting. Crystallizing. Fusing. Holding. Joining. Multiplying. Accreting. Bridging. Caulking. Fissuring. Hitting. Windblasting. Torquing. Wedging. Wrinkling. Splintering. Rubbing. Affixing. Banding. Combining. Cracking. Chipping. Damaging. Decomposing. Building. Spinning. Repelling. Attracting. Banging. Freezing. Warming. Aligning. Breaking. Collapsing. Flowing. Snowing. Rotating.

Sliding. Radiating. Shooting. Settling. Applying. Arranging. Fragmenting. Splitting. Braiding. Attenuating. Burning. Flaking. Crumbling. Avalanching. Buttressing. Fracturing. Bouncing. Furrowing. Drip. Drip. Blip. Blup.

Erupting. Evaporating. Annealing. Adhering. Bending. Leaning. Receding. Denting. Growing. Evolving. Hurling. Integrating. Jolting. Flaring. Melting. Melding. Decaying. Exploding. Shoving. Separating. Tripping. Vibrating. Weathering. Opening. I was a traveler from another galaxy, a military and space-program pilot highly trained in science, sent on a mission to find a suitable place to where my planet's population might be conveyed before our impending certain extermination when our own sun would collapse, like all stars (including yours) will at some time when their fuel burns out. When that unfortunate incident occurs, the star begins to expand, its surface temperature cools down, and it glows red. The star grows so large that it encroaches on the orbits of the planets closest to it. When it reaches my own planet, it occupies about half the sky above. The air heats up so that the oceans boil and water evaporates and all life gets vaporized. My planet becomes engulfed and then evaporates into a puff of smoke. Our society was highly advanced in technology and knowledge but a little behind in the project to find another planet on which to relocate. I was one of two women making up the team of seven explorers. We were sent, each in our own space car, into very different neighborhoods of the universe. Plying. Pushing. Pulling. Ripping. Pinching. Oozing. Rotting. Slicing. Sanding. Scraping. Abutting. Crystallizing. Fusing. Holding. Joining. Multiplying. Accreting. Bridging. Caulking. Fissuring. Hitting. Windblasting. Torquing. Wedging. Wrinkling. Splintering. Rubbing. Affixing. Banding. Combining. Cracking. Chipping. Damaging. Decomposing. Building. Spinning. Repelling. Attracting. Banging. Freezing. Warming. Aligning. Breaking. Collapsing. Flowing. Snowing. Rotating. Sliding. Radiating. Shooting. Settling. Applying. Arranging. Fragmenting. Splitting. Braiding. Attenuating. Burning. Flaking. Crumbling. Avalanching. Buttressing. Fracturing. Bouncing. Furrowing.

Erupting. Evaporating. Annealing. Adhering. Bending. Crunching. Plummeting. Denting. Growing. Evolving. Hurling. Integrating. Jolting. Flaring. Melting. Melding. Decaying. Exploding. Shoving. Separating. Tripping. Vibrating. Weathering. Opening. Plying. Pushing. Pulling. Ripping. Voyages through vast space require time. If you were to travel in an aircraft going 550 miles per hour, it would take five hours to get across the continental United States. It would take eighteen days to get to the moon. To arrive at the sun would require twenty years of travelling. It would take eighty-two years to get to Jupiter and seven-hundred fifty years to Pluto. To arrive at the nearest star would require five million years of travelling. Without getting into all the scientific advances and technologies my planet's people had devised, suffice it to say that we had found ways to shorten these travel times substantially, thus making it possible for me to arrive here. But it still took a lot of time. Pinching. Oozing. Rotting. Slicing. Sanding. Scraping. Abutting. Crystallizing. Fusing. Holding. Joining. Multiplying. Accreting. Bridging. Caulking. Fissuring. Hitting. Windblasting. Torquing. Wedging. Wrinkling. Splintering. Rubbing. Affixing. Banding. Combining. Cracking. Chipping. Damaging. Decomposing. Building. Spinning. Repelling. Attracting. Banging. Freezing. Warming. Aligning. Breaking. Collapsing. Flowing. Snowing. Rotating. Sliding. Radiating. Shooting. Settling. Applying. Arranging. Fragmenting. Splitting. Braiding. Attenuating. Burning. Flaking. Crumbling. Avalanching. Buttressing. Fracturing. Bouncing. Furrowing.

Erupting. Evaporating. Annealing. Adhering. Bending. Ledging. Reaming. Denting. Growing. Evolving. Hurling. Integrating. Jolting. Flaring. Melting. Melding. Decaying. Exploding. Shoving. Separating. Tripping. Vibrating. Weathering. Opening. Plying. Pushing. Pulling. Ripping. Pinching. Oozing. Rotting. Slicing. Sanding. Scraping. Abutting. Crystallizing. Fusing.

Holding. As I think you know, it cannot be surprising that life can exist on planets other than Earth. With so many stars and their planets in the universe, there had to be a good chance that at least some of those could present conditions suitable to sustain life. If you were to look through the lens of the Hubble telescope and select a tiny point in the sky the size of 1/100 the area of a full moon, you could discern thousands of galaxies in that miniscule pinpoint! Thousands! Then, if you were to look closer, you could find that within each galaxy are one-hundred billion stars! Now, if you then scanned all the other pinpoints in the entire sky, you could discover that there are fifty-to-one-hundred billion galaxies in the universe! If you then were to multiply the number of stars in a galaxy by the number of galaxies, you would arrive at there being one sextillion stars in the world, each of which could have orbiting planets. That number is a one followed by twenty-one zeros, written as 1,000,000,000,000,000,000,000! There are more stars than grains of sand lying on all the beaches on planet Earth! And out of all those planets that are out there, could at least one or two, at a minimum, have conditions that are conducive to supporting life? Well, my planet was one of them. Orbiting. Joining. Multiplying. Accreting. Bridging. Caulking. Fissuring. Hitting. Windblasting. Torquing. Wedging. Wrinkling. Splintering. Rubbing. Affixing. Banding. Combining.

Cracking. Chipping. Damaging. Decomposing. Building. Spinning. Repelling. Attracting. Banging. Freezing. Warming. Aligning. Breaking. Collapsing. Flowing. Snowing. Rotating. Sliding. Radiating. Shooting. Settling. Applying. Arranging. Fragmenting. Splitting. Braiding. Attenuating. Burning. Flaking. Crumbling. Avalanching. Buttressing. Fracturing. Bouncing. Furrowing.

Erupting. Evaporating. Annealing. Adhering. Bending. Leaking. Reforming. Denting. Growing. Evolving. Hurling. Integrating. Jolting. Flaring. Melting. Melding. Decaying. Exploding. Shoving. Separating. Tripping. Vibrating. Weathering. Opening. Plying. Pushing. Pulling. Ripping. Pinching. Oozing. Rotting. Slicing. Sanding. Scraping. Abutting. Crystallizing. Fusing. Holding. Joining. Multiplying. Accreting. Bridging. Caulking. Fissuring. Hitting. Windblasting. As one of the first space travelers to go this far, I was faced with unforeseen glitches. There were the little things, like the time I scraped my knee badly on a jagged rock while climbing on the earth's surface. It took a while to mend properly. I had adequate medical resources, but that particular wound was especially dangerous because of the nature of the infection. Fortunately it healed okay. Another time, I caught some kind of bug and was ill for a stretch, and very glad when I shook that off. But the two most searing glitches of all were, first of all, the one that prevented me from returning to my galaxy. I was completely stuck where I was with absolutely no chance of navigating myself back. I could only hope that someday help would arrive to take me back home again. At least, even though the space car could not make the crossing to return to my planet, it could, and did, serve me well as it functioned in a local, relatively restricted environment in the vicinity of the planet. The second major problem occurred when I lost all communication with my home. This happened a few years following the realization that I would be incapable of returning home on my own. Now there was no one to even talk to. Oh well, I thought, stuff happens. At least I had my cat to keep me company. Torquing. Wedging. Wrinkling. Splintering. Rubbing. Affixing. Banding. Combining. Cracking. Chipping. Damaging. Decomposing. Building. Spinning. Repelling. Attracting. Banging. Freezing. Warming. Aligning. Breaking. Collapsing. Flowing. Snowing. Rotating. Sliding. Radiating. Shooting. Settling. Applying. Arranging. Fragmenting. Splitting. Braiding. Attenuating. Burning. Flaking. Crumbling. Avalanching. Buttressing. Fracturing. Bouncing. Furrowing.

Erupting. Evaporating. Annealing. Adhering. Bending. Nudging. Surging. Denting. Growing. Evolving. Hurling. Integrating. Jolting. Flaring. Melting. Melding. Decaying. Exploding. Shoving. Separating. Tripping.

Vibrating. Weathering. Opening. Plying. Pushing. Pulling. Ripping. Pinching. Oozing. Rotting. Slicing. Sanding. Scraping. Abutting. Crystallizing. Fusing. Holding. Joining. Multiplying. Accreting. Bridging. Caulking. Fissuring. Hitting. Windblasting. Torquing. People in our society had evolved to a point in which our lifespans were incredibly long. And because of my participation in the space program, my own lifespan was medically increased even more. I was five foot seven inches tall and, because of our slow aging, looked like I was only thirty years of age on Earth. Our people looked pretty similar to earthlings, but there were some minor differences, such as the fact that we had lost those troublesome, no-longer-necessary third molar teeth eons ago. Wedging. Wrinkling. Splintering. Rubbing. Affixing. Banding. Combining. Cracking. Chipping. Damaging. Decomposing. Building. Spinning. Repelling. Attracting. Banging. Freezing. Warming. Aligning. Breaking. Collapsing. Flowing. Snowing. Rotating. Sliding. Radiating. Shooting. Settling. Applying. Arranging. Fragmenting. Splitting. Braiding. Attenuating. Burning. Flaking. Crumbling. Avalanching. Buttressing. Fracturing. Bouncing. Furrowing.

Erupting. Evaporating. Annealing. Adhering. Bending. Nipping. Scintillating. Denting. Growing. Evolving. Hurling. Integrating. Jolting. Flaring. Melting. Melding. Decaying. Exploding. Shoving. Separating.

Tripping. Vibrating. Weathering. Opening. Plying. Pushing. I admit there were a few times I regretted volunteering for this mission. I became angry sometimes— "Why did this stupid equipment have to fail and leave me stranded like this with no one to talk to? Did something in the system back home malfunction to screw me over? Was it human error? Was somebody distracted from his or her job because of being too busy texting friends during work hours?" Then, after the anger had subsided, I would settle down, shrug my shoulders, and ground myself and remember that "unforeseen glitches can occur in this world and so, oh well, just get on." Pulling. Ripping. Pinching. Oozing. Rotting. Slicing. Sanding. Scraping. Abutting. Crystallizing. Fusing. Holding. Joining. Multiplying. Accreting. Bridging. Caulking. Fissuring. Hitting. Windblasting. Torquing. Wedging. Wrinkling. Splintering. Rubbing. Affixing. Banding. Combining. Cracking. Chipping. Damaging. Decomposing. Building. Spinning. Repelling. Attracting. Banging. Freezing. Warming. Aligning. Breaking. Collapsing. Flowing. Snowing. Rotating. Sliding. Radiating. Shooting. Settling. Applying. Arranging. Fragmenting. Splitting. Braiding. Attenuating. Burning. Flaking. Crumbling. Avalanching. Buttressing. Fracturing. Bouncing. Furrowing.

Erupting. Evaporating. Annealing. Adhering. Bending. Nicking. Upthrusting. Denting. Growing.

Evolving. Hurling. Integrating. Jolting. Flaring. Melting. Melding. Decaying. Exploding. Shoving. Separating. Tripping. Vibrating. Weathering. Opening. Plying. Pushing. Pulling. Ripping. Pinching. Oozing. Rotting. Slicing. Sanding. Scraping. Abutting. Crystallizing. Fusing. Holding. Joining. Multiplying. Accreting. Bridging. Caulking. Fissuring. Hitting. I've . . . I've . . . had to develop a supreme degree of total patience . . . to survive . . . under these extreme circumstances of . . . being isolated . . . from . . . other people. I miss my grownup children, so very much. I miss . . . my husband, an accomplished soul, who was always unselfishly supportive of me. I miss him so much. So much, you just don't know. Just before I entered the spacecraft for liftoff, I will never forget how he said, "I will see you very soon." I answered, "I love you always" and will remember forever the sad look he inadvertently flashed back to me as he tried unsuccessfully to hide the uncertainty. His eyes said it all. Well, we knew the risks involved. My spacecraft lifted off from the launch pad and I never saw him again, except for the initial video communications. In the early years following the launch of this space jaunt, every year I would foolishly smear on lipstick and get all dressed up on our marriage anniversary, as if I had a date and was heading out for a romantic dinner after which I would do wild things with the man I loved.

Now I felt as if I was entombed, locked into slow time, embedded completely within a rock world. At least the food supply loaded onto my space capsule was endless and quite adequate, and able to be stored and preserved successfully to last billions of years. Being enclosed as I was within this rocky existence upon the planet, thoroughly encased by physical and chemical processes, at least I was still alive and had not yet turned into a fossil. Windblasting. Torquing. Wedging. Wrinkling. Splintering. Rubbing. Affixing. Banding. Combining. Cracking. Chipping. Damaging. Decomposing. Building. Spinning. Repelling. Attracting. Banging. Freezing. Warming. Aligning. Breaking. Collapsing. Flowing. Snowing. Rotating. Sliding. Radiating. Shooting. Settling. Applying. Arranging. Fragmenting. Splitting. Braiding. Attenuating. Burning. Flaking. Crumbling. Avalanching. Buttressing. Fracturing. Bouncing. Furrowing.

Erupting. Evaporating. Annealing. Adhering. Bending. Overtaking. Upheaving. Denting. Growing. Evolving. Hurling. Integrating. Jolting. Flaring. Melting. Melding. Decaying. Exploding. Shoving. Separating. Tripping. Vibrating. Weathering. Opening. Plying. Pushing. Pulling. Ripping. Pinching. Oozing. Rotting. Slicing. Sanding. Scraping. Abutting. Why did I volunteer for this project anyway? Well, I knew I was qualified and could make a difference in the fate of our planet. I was in great physical condition. There was a sense of duty, a profound responsibility. There was the terrible thought that everything could be lost forever. Think of it in this way: it was the same as if your sun was about to collapse and you would have to face the prospect of losing everything on your planet. All the great accomplishments—Beethoven's symphonies, Wagner's operas, Shakespeare's plays, Van Gogh's paintings, *Abbey Road*, *Thus Spake Zarathustra*, the *Turangalila Symphony*, the great buildings and bridges, the inventions and medical advances that helped make life easier—would be lost forever, like they never happened. Such a horrifying thought, the impermanence of it all! I wondered if any of the other pilots were successful in finding a suitable place to live. Did my planet's population survive? Were the people moved to a new world, or did they suffer a heart-wrenching demise? Crystallizing. Fusing. Holding. Joining. Multiplying. Accreting. Bridging. Caulking. Fissuring. Hitting. Windblasting. Torquing. Wedging. Wrinkling. Splintering. Rubbing. Affixing. Banding. Combining. Cracking. Chipping. Damaging. Decomposing. Building. Spinning. Repelling. Attracting. Banging. Freezing. Warming. Aligning. Breaking. Collapsing. Flowing. Snowing. Rotating. Sliding. Radiating. Shooting. Settling. Applying. Arranging. Fragmenting. Splitting. Braiding. Attenuating.

Burning. Flaking. Crumbling. Avalanching. Buttressing. Fracturing. Bouncing. Furrowing.

Erupting. Evaporating. Annealing. Adhering. Bending. Pervading. Grating. Denting. Growing. Evolving. Hurling. Integrating. Jolting. Flaring. Melting. Melding. Decaying. Exploding. Shoving. Separating. Tripping. Vibrating. Weathering. Opening. Plying. Pushing. Pulling. Ripping. Pinching. Oozing. Rotting. Slicing. Sanding. Scraping. Abutting. Crystallizing. Fusing. Holding. Joining. Multiplying. Accreting. Bridging. Caulking. Fissuring. Hitting. Windblasting. Torquing. Wedging. Wrinkling. Splintering. Rubbing. Affixing. Banding. Combining. Cracking. Chipping. Damaging. There was one other glitch: Everything that came with me from my planet, including my cat and myself and the space car, began shrinking a few thousand years ago. It was some kind of a reaction in which we began devolving into less mass. Don't ask me to explain how metal shrinks and how it gets smaller at an equal and consistent rate with everything else that I brought along with me from my planet! That's a complex one. Not long after humans entered the scene on Earth, this stranded space traveler became small like a dragonfly. Then, later, the size of a mosquito, to get even tinier as time went along. Pretty absurd, I know. But nevertheless, despite the shrinking, I was still able to get a great view of human history because I could travel all over the planet just as quickly as before. You wouldn't believe how fast I could drive that space car around, the way I used to rev up that engine. Decomposing. Building. Spinning. Repelling. Attracting. Banging. Freezing. Warming. Aligning. Breaking. Collapsing. Flowing. Snowing. Rotating. Sliding. Radiating. Shooting. Settling. Applying. Arranging. Fragmenting. Splitting. Braiding. Attenuating. Burning. Flaking. Crumbling. Avalanching. Buttressing. Fracturing. Bouncing. Furrowing.

Erupting. Evaporating. Annealing. Adhering. Bending. Denting. Growing. Evolving. Hurling. Integrating. Jolting. Flaring. Melting. Melding. Decaying. Exploding. Shoving. Separating. Tripping. Vibrating. Weathering. Opening. Plying. Pushing. Pulling. Ripping. Pinching. Oozing. Rotting. Slicing. Sanding. Scraping. Abutting. Crystallizing. Fusing. Holding. Joining. Multiplying. Accreting. Bridging. Caulking. Fissuring. Hitting. Windblasting. Torquing. Wedging. Wrinkling. Splintering. Rubbing. Affixing. Banding. Combining. Cracking. Chipping. Damaging. Decomposing. Building. Spinning. Repelling. Attracting. Banging. Freezing. Warming. Aligning. Breaking. Collapsing. Flowing. Snowing. Rotating. Sliding. Radiating. Shooting. Settling. Applying. Arranging. Fragmenting. Splitting. Braiding.

Attenuating. Burning. Flaking. Crumbling. Avalanching. Buttressing. Fracturing. Bouncing. Furrowing.

Erupting. Evaporating. Annealing. Adhering. Bending. Denting. Growing. Evolving. Hurling. Integrating. Jolting. Flaring. Melting. Melding. Decaying. Exploding. Shoving. Separating. Tripping. Vibrating. Weathering. Opening. Plying. Pushing. Pulling. Ripping. Pinching. Oozing. Rotting. Slicing. Sanding. Scraping. Abutting. Crystallizing. Fusing. Holding. Joining. Multiplying. Accreting. Bridging. Caulking. Fissuring. Hitting. Windblasting. Torquing. Wedging. Wrinkling. Splintering. Rubbing. Affixing. Banding. Combining. Cracking. Chipping. Damaging. Decomposing. Building. Spinning. Repelling. Attracting. Banging. Freezing. Warming. Aligning. Breaking. Collapsing. Flowing. Snowing. Rotating. Sliding. Radiating. Shooting. Settling. Applying. Arranging. Fragmenting. Splitting. Braiding. Attenuating. Burning. Flaking. Crumbling. Avalanching. Buttressing. Fracturing. Bouncing. Furrowing.

Thus the dirt-colored, blue-infused world I witnessed was one of turmoil and change, natural forces blowing and burning and washing out the landscape, of rocks and dirt getting moved around over vast lapses of time in a harsh, rugged, precarious, and often unforgiving terrain that moved continually through space. It was a hostile, perilous place—not a home a person creating a happy fairy tale would construct, no garden of Eden. Regardless, it was as it was, the home that was given.

Then, sometime before three-and-a-half billion years ago: gentle, delicate life emerged for the first time here.

The ingredients that would be necessary to make this possible had somehow come together just right in a fortuitous way—it seemed to me it was a miracle anything here could be alive at all. It presented in the form of simple entities intimately interacting with the dangerous physical environment of the planet in their quest to function and thrive. Subsequently, the game of evolution played out as more species appeared. Creatures found themselves up against the falling debris from the sky, the tectonic shifts of underground boulders, and the forces of weathering. They had to contend with disease, predators, famines, parasites, and storms. It was a game of the survival of the fittest. More and more complex life forms would slowly follow, including humans, who would come and add to this shaky place even more pain, cruelty, and misery, and beauty and love and kindness.

TWO

Bright orange flowers with petals the size of automobile tires and spotted stalks nine feet tall adorned the ancient earth. Scattered among these were skinny yellow champagne glass flowers. Lush green spider fern palms waved gently in the warm breeze. Red and brown reeds formed a dense mat around the periphery of the immediate, colorful landscape. A succulent olive-green plant with teeth, like a Venus flytrap, snapped and caught a fly that had the same wingspan as a canary. Monkeys chattered from the treetops. Elephant-like creatures trumpeted bellicosely. Green lizards scurried and multicolored snakes slithered. The golden sun beamed down its blinding rays. The enormous sky was deep blue and there was at present no rush hour of fluffy snowy clouds passing through. It was the morning of a new day, inundated and saturated with vibrant, variegated life.

Koobi, the largest and strongest of the clan, pointed inland to a dormant volcano and the rest of the group looked. He was excited about a large black boulder protruding from the eastern slope of the leviathan cinder cone, which had not hurled lava for five months now. Koobi made gestures that emphasized how impressed he was that the rock had not yet been broken loose to roll down the steep incline.

Tica, a middle-aged woman twelve years old, recalled a similar landmark carved out of a different lava-hurler which had been agitated by attention-getting earth tremors, and which bounced and crashed down to the flat plain below while resonating loudly so all could hear. That protuberance had not lasted very long before making its descent. In that way it differed greatly from the black stone that Koobi currently focused upon.

Koobi laughed, thinking how stubborn that lump of rock was, and then stopped to silently and carefully admire this testament to strength and perseverance. Here was a durable rock, he acknowledged.

Someone yelled and all heads turned in the opposite direction, where the ocean waves pounded the shoreline of what would someday be called East Africa. From the slightly elevated promontory, the adults were able to keep watch over the clan's ten children who were playing and enjoying themselves on the sandy beach.

The older children were directing the activities. Oldu, a boy with one arm slightly longer than the other, had just finished constructing a "mountain" out of sand. Uvai imitated him and put together a mountain, too, but then pushed his fist through its peak to create what he declared to be a volcano crater.

Another child made barely audible singing-like noises. She had just recently become homeless, on account of her entire family having been wiped out one day when the ground split open and swallowed them down while the girl clung desperately to a sturdy deep-rooted tree. She was pulled up by Koobi, who happened to be walking near, onto stable turf. The clan decided to adopt her because they felt sorry for her and the predicament into which she had been cast.

The girl carved a furrow into the sand, into which tidewater from the ocean swarmed. Ser, another girl who was the same age as the adopted girl, cried out happily that it looked like a river now! The two little girls laughed together. The waves soon encroached, however, and washed away the banks of their river and so Ser and the girl had to rebuild.

After the children finished constructing a more extensive miniature landscape of mountains, rivers, plateaus, and volcanoes, Oldu stomped his feet and cried out that an earthquake was hitting. "Stop it!" demanded

Ser, "You are breaking everything!" Oldu was nice and so he stopped.

They carved a cave out of one of the mountains, trying to duplicate the one in which the clan lived much of the time. They used rocks of different sizes to bolster the walls and ceiling of the structure. The kids brought shells filled with saltwater. One univalve was as large and as deep as a jumbo mailbox.

Eti was best at forming the white sand. He knew how to work it and was fast at building things. He had it all figured out as to just how wet to get a handful of sand so it would effectively stick and stay put to a larger pile of sand when he carefully patted it into place just right.

One boy with hair longer and darker than the other children farted, and all the kids laughed, except for Tanza, who simultaneously stubbed her toe on a half-hidden piece of beige driftwood, which made her cry for a minute. She recovered and continued playing.

A few different species of seaweed lay scattered on the beach. One of the boys, named Eng, picked up a long green slimy one and threw it at two of his playmates who were stooped over a horseshoe crab. The seaweed landed across their backs. They cried out and retrieved the weed and hurled it back at the instigator. Before long, all became engaged in the frolic. Other types of colorful sea plants that had been previously washed ashore, some red, some bluish, became objects of their sport and were tossed around.

Someone splashed water by kicking her foot into an incoming swell. Ser got water in her eyes and splashed back. Now the game had become a splashfest as the kids ran all around the beach playing. Tanza hurled water in Eti's face, causing Eti to get water up his nose. He did not like that and so he reached out and pulled Tanza's long hair on her hirsute arm. Tanza retaliated by pulling Eti's thick, curly hair on his back and abdomen. In the end, they all laughed at each other, rolling in the sand.

In time, the seven adults strode down to join the children. They watched them play, reminiscing about the days they did the same.

The three adult males in the clan huddled together around a large granite boulder that was splashed occasionally by the incoming waves. Ever since their chance encounter in Laetoli with the strange clan last year when the summer was in full swing, their minds were wandering up and down, and side to side, as they tried to devise a new strategy. They had witnessed a man from that tribe run swiftly enough across the open plain to actually catch and wrestle down a small antelope. Never had they seen this before.

They were amazed by what they observed. They puzzled over its meaning since, but never more so than today, with the surf incessantly marching in and then out, calling out its rhythmic, mesmerizing chant, alternating between raucous and pianissimo, and never relenting.

"I think they watched for days and picked out the weakest," offered Ponga.

"And ran it down and used a sharp stone to end it," suggested Koobi.

"It could not be easy," mused Punga.

As they discussed these matters three-and-a-half million years ago in Africa, these human ancestors were not yet at the level of development where their descendents would be with regard to the ability to talk. Their vocal mechanisms were not fully formed. Communication was, nevertheless, successfully accomplished by eye movements, noises and limited guttural pronouncements, and hand and body gestures. They did not speak the languages of modern humans, but were able to effectively understand one another, and if someone foreign to them was patient and spent time with them, he or she would find it possible as well to figure out their communicative methods and be able to relate to them.

It was about six-million years before this discussion that currently occurred among Koobi, Punga, and Ponga when one of their ancestors made the bold move to come down out of the trees to spend increasingly more time on the ground. In the trees, things were comfortable. There they could munch on leaves and catch insects to eat. Their arms and legs were much longer then, enabling them to maneuver efficiently through the arboreal environment. They were as adept as little squirrels getting around, grasping bark and propelling themselves from branch to branch. They were tree creatures, and had been for a great long time. But when their ancestor journeyed to the soil and remained there for longer and longer durations, a groundbreaking precedent had been established. Other individuals occasionally followed.

But each time they made the dangerous move of climbing down to the ground, these people risked getting attacked and eaten by one or more of the many terrestrial predators who ruled and lurked in the shadows. Nonetheless, this potentially suicidal act unfolded from time to time because curiosity drove some to attempt this, to see what was down there.

One of the rewards, however, of leaving the tree was the acquisition of fruits and vegetables that were not accessible from the tree. These could be gathered and eaten on the ground or brought back to the home. The menu was expanded.

There were times in the night when lions killed their prey and the tree creatures listened. There was the growl and the movement of bodies through the brush. After the chase abruptly ended, the food feast began and smells of the slaughter wafted up to the trees, where the tree-dwellers sensed it.

At some point one of the braver tree-dwellers, drawn by the commotion and perhaps enticed by the culinary potential, snuck down and proceeded on all four limbs to the scraps left behind. Gnawing on the bones, a new addition to the customary diet was discovered. It was a momentous event, and this maneuver became habitual to this creature. Eventually some bones and meat scraps were brought back to the tree to be shared. Perhaps two or three souls waited near the bottom of the trunk, or maybe the food would be brought to the canopy high above.

As the trips down from the tree became more frequent, word got around and more were willing to try it. Scavenging had begun to become an accepted means of obtaining food. But it was dangerous, and many deaths occurred when the tree creatures became the prey of the waiting terrestrial carnivores, unable to scurry away on all four extremities to a safe place. The advantage went to whoever was faster and better at sensing when a predator neared.

Then one day a Great One stood up on two legs only. He fell, though, but with determination continued trying to remain upright. Despite being derided by the skeptics and falling countless more times, he at last was able to adopt a bipedal posture and maintain it. Bipedalism in this species was invented and he insisted it was the ticket to finer dining. He believed in its value to future generations. He coaxed and recruited interested tree climbers. He became a coach of sorts, demonstrating the technique and drilling a formation of tree creatures on the ground under the tree, like an instructor in an aerobics class at a gym. "Stand up straight, I said! That's it; you'll get it if you keep trying!" In time, more of these primates were able to walk on two limbs.

Then, in time, the same individual or some other innovator was able to coordinate leg movements so to make it possible to run. This advancement enabled the scavengers to flee and escape predators much more effectively when they were threatened.

Thereafter, scavenging and the gathering of food from the ground was the name of the game, added to the traditional catching of insects and munching on leaves in the trees. This way of life persisted for six-million years, returning us once again to the clan members who were having their discussions while huddled upon that rock alongside the ocean's roaring waves.

While the ocean's surf tugged at their legs and whispered in their ears, Koobi, Punga, and Ponga made a decision that one of them would attempt to run down an antelope. They wanted to move into new territory, into the start of more aggressive ways of obtaining sustenance.

The time was right. Their food supply was diminished this past year. They needed to try, and now was the time. Punga was fastest, but weakest. Koobi, the wise elder to whom the others deferred and respected highly, was slowest, but strongest. Ponga, who was Punga's younger brother, was in the middle regarding skills and everyone agreed he should attempt to capture an antelope first. This act would require courage, because he could get gored by an antler, or kicked hard enough that he could die. Ponga had a lot to think about now that he was selected.

The children were summoned from the beach to follow the adults up the slope to walk to the customary place for dinner. Arriving there, they set out to eat. Earlier in the day, fresh berries had been gathered and placed into a large, flat bivalve half-shell, which now was passed around so the clan could share the delicious food. They sat on the dirt and grass, the crashing surf heard unwaveringly although muffled because of the now greater distance from its raging edge. A mild wind blew and the sun's heat found its way down to the summer ground. The women had gathered edible leaves and now everyone enjoyed eating the salad.

Early in the morning the men had picked clams from the littoral zone. A strong, sharp piece of wood was used to pry the shell open to get at the meat within. Nothing was wasted. All of them were sure to scrape off the adductor muscle by sliding the fingernail under the cylindrical-shaped part of the clam. Over time, their fingernails grew very strong and thick and were useful adjuncts to be used for completing many of the daily tasks required for survival, which included an occasional back scratch.

In addition to obtaining clams, there were slow fish which the men were able to catch with their bare hands as they waded in the water when it rained earlier in the morning. "Good time to catch fish," declared Koobi.

They had all these foods at their disposal, but the quantity of each was limited, in small portions, inadequate for the long haul.

Because of their preoccupation with running down an antelope, the men reminisced more about that Laetoli valley, where they had once lived, and where they first got the idea of this kind of hunting. For many years they had dwelled there in that peaceful place, but then relocated east, albeit reluctantly, when the food supply there thinned out.

Ponga, between mouthfuls of fish, recalled how one day he and Punga stooped low in the Laetoli brush to hide as two adults and a child australopithecine strode by. The adult australopithecines were short in stature, only four feet six inches tall, with arms much longer than the arms of Punga and Ponga and hands straighter and less curved. They were bipeds and walked with a rolling gait on a dry riverbed through freshly deposited soft volcanic ash, which looked like snow and had been softened into a mud by a sprinkle of rain that had followed the ash's deposition on the ground. The older prehumans walked abreast of each other while the child playfully stepped inside one of the adult's footprints. The adults left prints that were smaller than modern humans and very apelike, but resembled more advanced humans in that the toes were longer and more spread apart, the arches were well-developed, and the big toes were not so much off to the side as they are in apes. They moved with a slow, rolling gait, with the hips swiveling upon every step forward, proceeding in a generally straight line. More ash descended from the sky later in the day, settling over the by-now hardened footprints. The evidence of the bipeds' path remained etched in the land along an eighty-foot stretch after the sun baked it in the subsequent weeks while Koobi, Punga, and Ponga lived in the region. They and the women and children of their clan often visited the site to marvel at the lasting image.

Ponga remembered the volcanic eruption that came shortly before those australopithecines traversed the field. It was a particularly violent one. The ashes covered the plain. The lava flowed in the direction of the sacred tree, a very important landmark to them, located about three-hundred yards closer to the volcano from the field where the australopithecines had strode. It would not have been good if the lava reached the shrine and so the two men scrambled to dig a primitive trench around it, using crude stone tools and bare hands. Turning his neck to look back toward the volcano, Ponga saw the red-hot molten mass progressing slowly toward where they toiled feverishly. The tree was a unique tree, with its beautiful pattern of convoluted dark brown branches forming a honeycomb web of intrigue. They had spent countless moments gazing at the sacred tree, studying its meaning, in awe at its complex majesty. They took care to prune it and decorate the surroundings. Ponga even brought water from the nearby pond one drought-filled week to give it a drink before it might have shriveled.

The lava continued rolling in the tree's direction. Thunder and lightning flashed, and birds flew away while the ground shook. The two men dug more earth, trying desperately to form a moat around the god's altar. Then the lava reached the ditch. A few gallons of red-hot liquid dropped into the moat. The level rose higher. Eventually it was even with the top of the excavated furrow. Then the burning mass stopped its progression and went no further. The sacred tree was spared.

"What a day that was!" exclaimed Ponga.

"We worked hard!" answered Punga proudly.

"And we did not have *kotiko*," declared Ponga, which in their language meant something like fear, a fear that makes you soft. Kotiko was a state of mind that was not good in a harsh world that demanded hardness to survive.

The clan members passed the food around to each other. It was a somber scene as they sat around a circle, relishing every bite, chewing the morsels thoroughly. Periodically, one of them would leave the "table" to kneel at the stream that flowed swiftly and cold. They would cup their hands to scoop water, lifting it to their mouths to drink.

After everyone finished eating, Punga crept away from the clan like he usually did before bed. He moved with purpose along a roughly-emblazoned trail cut through the brush, arriving at a clearing where he crouched down and waited. The sky was overflowing with starry pinpoints of light. A soft zephyr gently blew through, waving his hair. It was a warm night. He waited patiently for someone who had become a dear, welcome presence each night for the past month.

Punga went to the same place where he had first seen a large animal, which he called a wolf-dog because it looked to him as if it had combined characteristics of the two kinds of animals, a month ago. Punga was very perceptive when it came to remembering faces and physical characteristics. They had initially spotted each other while walking alone on the trail, unknowingly approaching each other from opposite directions. Before converging, both stopped abruptly and froze in midstep. All defense mechanisms switched on as they studied each other, ready to fight or flee if necessary. Punga had a gentle way about him and when he relaxed and slowly lowered his body to the ground he sent a message to the animal that he meant no harm. The creature relaxed. But then a tree limb broke in the jungle and scared the wolf-dog away.

The next evening, however, both returned to the same place. They looked at each other from afar. Punga brought a piece of carrion meat that he smuggled from his family's dinner spread, scraps left behind by the hyenas and scavenged by the clan. Punga placed it on the ground, then stepped back several paces. The wolf hustled carefully over to the food and, accepting the gift, began eating it while looking up at Punga, on guard at all times. Almost every evening after that, the two would see each other again in the woods, most times in the absence of food. It was not food that attracted them. It was more so a sense of camaraderie. Over time, they both came to trust each other and so met closer together.

Now it was a month later following that first chance encounter, and on this evening Punga reached out and actually touched the wolf-dog, albeit briefly. The wolf-dog stayed and did not run. But at the same time, Punga was not naïve and so he carefully backed off to give the animal more space. They stared at each other, studying each other's physical features.

The wolf-dog saw that Punga, at four feet nine inches weighing about eighty-eight pounds with a slender build, was slightly taller than the average person. Punga's arms were much longer than his legs. His legs were angled inward at the thighs. His spine was more curved than those people who came before him, an evolutionary development that enabled him to absorb more shocks during the very biped act of walking upright. He was more apelike, however, than his descendents would be.

The wolf-dog discerned that, compared to an australopithecine, Punga's head was much higher and rounder, and the jaw smaller and less protruding. His hands were more curved, better suited for gripping, with an improved opposable thumb design, but still not developed enough to match the advanced design of Homo habilis. Punga's big toes were more in line with the other toes, not off to the sides as in the predecessors. His teeth were smaller than those of the australopithecines. Under his skin the skull bones were noticeably thinner since there was less need for thicker, stronger chewing muscles. His greatest asset was his mobility, which enabled him to escape predators by running. And of course the larger brain helped him think better.

Punga gazed at the wolf-dog, which must have weighed about one-hundred seventy-five pounds. He thought to himself, here is a beautiful and strong creature. He admired its long canine teeth and pointy molars. He saw these well when the animal yawned. The wolf-dog's tall, narrow ears rose upward from his face, angling slightly to the sides. The snout had a round black nose surrounded by a ring of white hair. The rest of his body was covered in brown and grey fur with white lower legs. Its claws were strong and long and to be respected. And its large furry paws rested beautifully flat against the green grass. Its bushy tail was about three feet long, wagging rapidly when he settled down and became more relaxed.

Of all the members in the clan, Punga possessed the most patience of all. He had a gentle manner that made anyone feel comfortable in his presence. He gave to this wild animal his unhurried time, gradually opening up communication. Who knew what another year of these friendly interactions could bring? Most individuals did not possess this degree of patience. They would immediately write off a person or animal that did not communicate in their own way, never allowing a relationship of genuine respect to arise. Instead, whoever was stronger and more aggressive would gain the upper hand. To Punga, animals and other prehumans were all the same and demanded respect. To him, they were all involved in a constant struggle to survive in a harsh land in an unforgiving life. There was a closeness of all the creatures that struggled here on this physical terrain. After all, it was not easy to persist here. Punga and Ponga's father died some time ago after being bitten by a venomous snake. Their mother passed away from a severe fever she contracted, for some reason unknown to them. Punga could never forget these losses.

Punga, who loved and respected the animals with whom he shared the earth, at times mourned when living things killed other living things for food. To him, it was a strange, unfair reality that saddened him deeply even though he understood its purpose in survival. But he still pounded his fist into the earth and angrily asked why life was as it was here.

Punga waved goodbye to the wolf-dog and made his way back to where the clan was gathered. When he arrived, the family had begun to retire for the night to the cave in the rocky cliffs along the ocean. Turka greeted him and told him Ponga had decided to hunt the antelope tomorrow morning. Standing at the spacious doorstep to their home, Ania and Kana, two women who remained outside to wait for Punga, gazed up at the stars, twinkling brightly in the benighted sky, and were thankful for all that they had as they thrived on planet Earth. Pausing a moment, a comfortable breeze blowing by, they then entered the opening in the earth, followed by Punga.

The cave was cool and offered relief from the heat. Once inside, they joined the rest of the group who were sitting in a circle. After Eti made everyone laugh when he made funny faces, pulling his earlobe one way while he held his mouth open in a crooked and humorous way, each went to his customary bed to sleep. Oldu lay down on the flattened rock surface, his head finding its place on a smooth part of the rock that was raised. The rock was his pillow. The rest of them did the same. This cave fortunately was bedecked with a sufficient number of these gentle rolling nooks.

The relatively closed spaces inside the cave smelled like the odors animals in a pen or a backyard shed overtaken by mice and squirrels would generate. The ceiling was not high at all so that in many places they had to duck. One rocky wall was moist, as water trickled down, sometimes producing a mild gurgling sound.

Uvai once found a disk-shaped rock that had a large round hole in its center. It had washed up on the beach, and he was so fascinated by it that he conveyed it to his bedside. He wondered what he could do with the strangely-shaped rock. He was able to insert a medium-sized branch from a tree through the hole, like a wheel axle. He thought, "I wish there was some way I could make another opening into this rock so I could stuff it with food and then roll it all around so I could deliver things to eat to people who had a hard time finding food." He pushed the stick through the hole and then, holding the ends of the stick began rolling the rock back and forth. When he announced this to everybody in the cave, some of the elders told him to discontinue his stupid ideas because he might get hurt. They told him to get to bed and go to sleep.

Koobi said, "Good sleep to all!" Then Oldu and Uvai said the same in unison, in their high-pitched little-boy voices. This was followed by Ser wishing that same salutation to all. Then it was Eng's turn and he decided to offer an alternative, "Good sleep to *everybody*!" The children giggled and some of the adults smiled. Eti found it necessary to add another variation, "To every*one*, good sleep!" Again there were laughs and a few smiles. They laughed so hard, one of them, possibly Eti, snorted. This continued a while until everyone had his or her chance to say good night. Then the youngest children began to get in repeats, giggling as they did so. And, after Oldu proclaimed, "Good sleep to everyone in caves!" followed by Uvai with "Good sleep to everybody in forests!" and Eng yelling loudly "Sleep good to all who are ocean swimming," the ritual became old and slightly annoying to most of the adults, and Tica, the adult who spent the most time watching over the kids, stepped in and demanded they all go to sleep when she yelled, "Okay! Okay! That's enough! Go to sleep!" The cave became quiet.

Punga lay with his spouse, Ania. They worshipped each other. They were truly soul mates. Two of the clan's children were theirs, sleeping nearby. Punga and Ania talked softly a while. For the first time, he told her about the wolf-dog. He had told no one about this before.

They sat up, facing each other. Punga stretched out his arms fully, his fingertips gently and barely touching Ania's face. Then, in silence, she lifted her hand to contact his fingertips, too, playfully pushing his arms back toward him. They played like this for a while, slowly moving back and forth, smiling while they remained focused as they stared into each other's eyes, barely blinking. Then Punga rubbed each side of her head, gently massaging her as her eyes closed. Both laid down entwined, enjoying each other's company. In time, both fell into a deep sleep.

The next day, dawn arrived and the men moved out for the hunt. They awakened to the sounds of birds chirping, rodents chattering, and the surf raging. The cooler nighttime air was now greeted by the warmth of the sun.

Ponga was ready to wrestle down an antelope. He had tossed and turned throughout the night thinking about the task. He did, however, acquire enough sleep to feel rested, despite being slightly nervous. He figured this was normal and then committed himself to doing what needed to be done.

The men moved into position along the edges of the wide open grassland. They knew they were entering a state-of-the-art, cutting-edge activity they had never engaged in before, filled with unknowns and uncertainties.

Koobi slapped Ponga on the butt and told him to "Go get it!"

Ponga smiled and declared, "I will!"

The men studied the situation and selected the animal Ponga would chase down. Ponga focused on it and began a mad dash. He caught it and wrestled it to the ground and tried to finish the task. The antelope's body writhed. What seemed an excessively long moment finally elapsed. Then the animal was able to regain its footing. It delivered a solid kick to Ponga's chest, knocking Ponga backward to the ground. The extricated ruminant looked back in victory before darting off uninjured.

The rest of the clan who had come along as bystanders ran to Ponga to see if he was all right. The wind appeared to be knocked out of him and a broad contusion began to form on his abdominal skin. He had a few minor scratches on his extremities. Ponga sat up from the ground and waved his hands in a way that reassured everyone he was fine. His stomach was aching a bit. He was more injured by his inability to close the deal. He had wanted to feel like he was on top of the world, but had failed.

The men and women consoled him. They said there was always another day to try again. Koobi agreed, but indicated that before that day would come, Punga would have his turn.

On the trek back to their cave, they fortuitously stumbled upon a lion's fresh kill. They attempted to drive the animal away so they could scavenge the meat, but were unsuccessful at first. After a few more tries, however, they were eventually victorious in scaring the lion away (or, perhaps more correctly, the animal had had its share and was satiated and became bored with all the attention the clan was giving to it), but found only a small portion of meat remaining. Nevertheless, at the least, this junior-sized quantity would nourish the clan sufficiently enough. They swiftly gathered what they could, before any other hungry creatures would come along.

The clan transported the meat to a place outside their cave, where they gathered and ate. They hauled the leftovers up a tall tree onto a thick, broad branch where they could store the foodstuffs high above ground so other scavengers would be less likely to get at it. The next day they noticed that the meat began to spoil and taste different. And on the third day they realized they could not eat anymore of it because of the poor condition of preservation it was in.

A week after the botched hunt, the adults swam in the ocean. They treaded water for a time, spinning and looking out further to sea, and admiring the view of the shoreline which was lined by huge and tall palm trees. They saw fish swim by. They saw jellyfish float near. They looked up at the blue sky with white puffy clouds moving slowly across.

That evening, Punga went to the trail to see if the wolf-dog would return. When he arrived at the usual meeting spot, there was no sign of the wild animal. Dusk had begun to set in. Giant black bats began patrolling the skies, devouring multitudes of airborne insects, using their radar to dart back and forth repeatedly. The roar of a tiger in the distance pierced the silence. Punga sat quietly, looking all around, picking at his nose. Frogs croaked.

The wolf-dog's shadow suddenly appeared on the ground ahead, scaring Punga as it took him by surprise. Punga said, "Well, hello, my friend." Punga had no food to bring to the wolf-dog today. The animal came right up to Punga, who was able to stroke his hand gently on his furry coat just to the rear of his neck. The wolf-dog rolled on his side. They looked at each other for some time. Punga slowly rested his forehead on the wolf-dog's, just above his eyes. They remained touching like this awhile. Punga could hear him breathing. They trusted each other.

Punga tossed a stick and the animal ran to it, picked it up between his teeth, and carried it back to Punga, dropping it on the ground before him. They played like this for some time, but then the wolf-dog stood at attention, looked at Punga, and ran away. It was characteristic of this wolf-dog to depart abruptly like this. Punga smiled and waited to see if it would return but when it did not, he turned and walked back to the camp.

In the morning, the children played in the stream that flowed to the blue ocean. Eti found a piece of floating driftwood stuck in a v-shaped notch created where two smooth grey rocks abutted one another. The current bubbled all around the brown wood, pushing it first to the right, then left, alternating like this while the four-inch diameter branch bobbled around, incapable of extricating itself from its trapped position. Eti watched it awhile. Then he lifted it out of the water. It was broad and flat-surfaced on one side. The other kids piled rocks on the oblate driftwood and then released it to float downstream. They followed its progress, watching curiously that its cargo remained intact, as they hiked along the stream bank. The current was slow. They came to a bend where thick vegetation would not permit them to remain streamside, so they had to cut through an opening of sparsely populated thin brush, knowing from familiarity with the region that it would lead them to a dirt path that would join again with the stream bank. When they arrived at the stream, Eng yelled and pointed, "Look! The rocks are still on top of the log!" They all smiled in fascination. Tanza jumped up in joy, her arms stretched upward toward the sunlit sky. The children followed the floating log to the beach where they watched it float into the surf.

On the beach, Oldu cried out a warning to the other children not to step on a pile of black obsidian fragments. He was exaggerating because these rocks were mostly smooth. He just knew from experience that sometimes they could be chipped to form sharp edges. Uvai picked up a few small pieces of the volcanic glass and shook them within his cupped-together hands, rattling the contents to produce a crisp sound. Eti got the idea of hitting two sticks like drumsticks against a downed tree trunk, generating percussive accents. Before long, he figured out a regular beat, while Uvai continued shaking the obsidian. Some of the other children crawled up on the thick tree trunk and began moving with the rhythm. Oldu noticed the drum sounds changed in timbre with each additional person who jumped onto the trunk. Tanza plucked a large umbrella-shaped flower from a shrub and wore it on her head like a hat. This made everybody laugh and some of the others jumped down from the tree trunk to run over to the shrub so they too could obtain headgear for themselves.

The whole time, Ania and Tica supervised the children, always on alert for unexpected predators. They had seen lions kill people before and were quite aware of the other perils that awaited out there. They knew they had to remain unceasingly vigilant.

When it was time to return to the clan's meeting place, the women summoned the children and everyone walked back along a trail, stopping to pick berries at one of their favorite bushes. Tica reached under the long leaves of the plant, retrieving a curved piece of dried bark that was hardened into the shape of a crude bowl. There were several more that she unveiled. These were kept here for their use whenever they needed more of the sweet purple fruit.

There were other people from different clans occupying the land to the immediate north and south of them. They did not interact much with these tribes, however, although on the few occasions in which they mingled, they found them to be friendly and good-natured. There was a kind of bond that these people had for one another in which they respected each other as they found themselves in a weary struggle for survival, as they carried out what they must do each day, sometimes looking bedraggled and war-torn but always attempting to elevate themselves with as much happiness as they could find.

A storm appeared suddenly. The benighted skies opened to unveil furious winds and driving, stinging rain. The clan sought shelter under trees, although everyone still got wet because of the storm's intensity. Thunder and lightning emerged, scaring the tiniest children, who clung tenaciously to the older individuals. Trees cracked and fell to the ground. The wind hurled hard objects, like coconuts, along the ground as projectiles. The swirling air was unkind to any living creatures that happened to get in its way. The clan huddled together and wondered when it would end.

In time, to their relief, the storm stopped raging, the rain lightened, and the thunder and lightning went back into hiding. Gradually everything returned to the calm that preceded nature's destructive, rearranging fury. Everyone was fine. No one was injured.

The next day, it was Punga's turn to catch an antelope. With mixed feelings he assented to the task. Koobi hugged Punga, wishing him luck. Punga answered, "I am not kotiko."

He chose the antelope that appeared to be the slowest. He began to run toward the animal. When he caught up with it he reached out and was able to get both his arms around it. Everything went as planned until the antelope moved its head in a violent way that enabled it to gore Punga in the abdomen, causing Punga to release his grip. He felt a sickly feeling come over his entire body. The antelope collapsed briefly but then sprung back up from the ground, blood flowing from the wound that was inflicted on its neck. It then limped away to rejoin the herd, apparently shook up but able to survive the challenge.

The clan ran to the site of carnage. When Koobi saw the wound on Punga, he knew immediately it was fatal and they could do nothing to save him. Ania arrived on the scene, screaming when she saw the injury to her spouse. One look at Koobi and she knew from his expression it was not good. She cradled Punga in her arms, hugging him tightly. Punga felt the blood rushing out from his body. He looked down and also knew what was to come.

"Did I live right?" he asked Ania. Not knowing up from down, right from wrong in her grief, she asked him what he meant. When he repeated the question, she only tried to reassure him and responded, "Yes, you did. You did. You did," and fell onto his lap sobbing uncontrollably.

"Did I live right? I just want to go home now," he cried.

"You will always be home with me, with everyone here. You are home, my dear," Ania said.

As Punga lay on his back, in pain with his knees bent, Ania knelt to his side. Punga grasped hands together with Ania.

Somewhere over the ridge an animal mournfully howled. Koobi looked in that direction, thinking he heard a wolf, and then signaled to Ponga to bring water for Punga to drink. When Ponga arrived back with the water, they noticed Punga had already taken his final breath. Ania collapsed on top of him, still holding onto his hands, their fingers interlocked.

THREE

During a long walk through storms and vast spans of slow time, where I witnessed the initially lifeless rocky terrain fill with primitive life-forms that evolved into more complex creatures, I came to understand there was an *unmistakable oneness*. And as Earth's history played out, I discovered a metaphorical road that could help explain this oneness and what to do with it, in effect helping to answer certain baffling questions that inhabitants of this planet had encountered over the centuries. These matters took me a long time to recognize, but when I did, it was clear. It was black and white.

*

The space car was a versatile and durable engineering marvel that enabled me to quite effectively observe human activity and everything else around me. I was aided by the advanced technology inherent in this particular spacecraft, a benefit that allowed me to get around. I thus witnessed people's actions and their discussions and debates as human history unfurled. Every day I was able to use this vehicle to visit all continents several times, if I desired, because of the high velocities I could attain when I pushed the Nomad to its utmost.

Fortunately, I could travel like this while inflicting minimal wear and tear on the mechanical components because of how well the craft was constructed. Of course, I also took the time to perform regular preventive maintenance and was highly trained to carry out any repairs when needed. Always, in the back of my mind, I remembered I had to keep this machine going for as long as I could. It had to last for many years, that being certainly an understatement, trapped as I was in my circumstances.

The elements of the Periodic Table always found ways to come together into a wide variety of inorganic arrangements. Inside the laboratory of this planet, given just the right mix of time, catalysts, and other conditions that included a bit of luck, eventually many of these compounds transposed into a thick black muck of organic compounds. Among these were amino acids, the building blocks of proteins which would become important parts of RNA and cell membranes. Strands of RNA and such formed a world of their own, running rampant throughout the bleak landscape, replicating and competing and leading to life based on DNA and genes capable of handing down more life to successive generations of living things, thus representing a common ancestor to everything that would follow. All of this was from some kind of Darwinian chemical evolution launched from the gas and dust of the planet and its surroundings.

The earliest, inaugural life emerged as anaerobic bacteria. One type lived around hot springs in the deepest parts of the ocean. Another kind was a cyanobacteria, a pond scum blue-green algae largely responsible for gradually increasing the amount of oxygen in the primeval atmosphere via photosynthesis. Thanks largely to this little creature, by two-and-a-half billion years ago enough oxygen existed in the atmosphere so that I no longer had to utilize the oxygen bubble technology. I was greatly relieved, given the degree of extra freedom.

The cyanobacteria created stromatolites—layered accretionary structures in shallow water formed by the trapping, binding, and cementation of sedimentary grains by biofilms created from the activities of the microorganisms. Many of these became laminated fossils, nonhuman archaeological landmarks commemorating incipient "heartbeats" here in this part of the universe.

Eventually, living cells became more complex when a simple unicellular creature wriggling through prokaryotic slime engulfed another and allowed it to continue to thrive as an organelle by setting up a symbiotic relationship and the first eukaryote.

Working together, some eukaryotes later became multicelled creatures. In the beginning, these animals were largely at the mercy of external forces, as they drifted and interacted only passively with the environment around them.

In time, these creatures would grow larger and sometimes sprout appendages and other devices. Living organisms would begin to actively interact with the planet by crawling over it, digging into it, or paddling through its water. Biomineralization would provide many of them with suits of protective armor. Sensory features such as eyes would develop, greatly assisting them as they navigated through the unforgiving environment.

I got to spend eons of time with prehistoric life. For the first millions of years, vital beings existed only in the oceans. I caught trilobites and let them swim a while in a large bucket filled with water. I waded in the ocean next to the Cambrian anomalocaris, with its three-foot long body, watching it search for food to seize, its two bulbous eyes sticking out to the sides on the termini of peduncles. Sometimes when one drifted past me in shallow water, its two spiny projections—which I describe as big stiff whiskers—would brush up against my leg, surprising me and inducing me to spin away in a mild panic.

Creatures came and went with waves of extinctions. It was as if the world with its big changes—in temperatures or chemical interactions or movements of its rocky foundations or upon being visited by factors such as gamma rays or asteroids from outer space—was experimenting with a wide variety of body designs, conceptions that were often wildly bizarre, to be discarded periodically in an attempt to create better technical products more suited to surviving on the fluctuating planet. I held a spindly little hallucinogenia in the palm of my hand and said to it, "My goodness, people in the future might have a hard time orienting you!"

During the Devonian Period, I could very well have become a world class fisherwoman if I wanted because of the great number and variety of fish that were out and about. I often watched primitive sharks patrolling near the shoreline, their dorsal fins cutting a trail through the surface of the water. One hot morning I caught a steely-blue coelacanth fish with my rod and reel. It took me by surprise, as I had believed it to be already extinct. As I released it into the water, I reassured it that I would not write it off again, although I could give no guarantees that other fishermen would do the same.

Then during the Silurian period, mossy plants began to live in damp areas near the water's edge. Around four-hundred million years ago, the hardscrabble land magically transformed, becoming green when a plethora of plants of all shapes and sizes emerged to cover the place with thick vegetation. My aerial reconnaissance trips in the space car now revealed various shades of this new color covering widespread tracts of the formerly exclusively rocky, barren, and dirty landscape. It was like all of the land had become one big green Ireland celebrating a happy Saint Patrick's day to all.

Also thriving during the Silurian period were twenty-six foot tall prototaxites that projected upward like Egyptian obelisks scattered randomly over the ground. These were odd giant fungus conglomerations that could be thirty feet tall and three feet wide, presenting like upright tree trunks without branches or leaves. I just mused, "What's the point?"

Eventually, creatures moved onto the land. One day as I was walking along a lake shore, a seven-foot-long amphibian called eryops appeared ahead of my path. It opened its mouth widely to display its sharp teeth which were suitable for eating meat. It then shut its mouth, looked at me, took a step toward the water but then reversed course and took two steps back inland. It then hesitated and repeated that fancy footwork. It was as if it were saying, "Should I stay here or should I go there?" In the end, as it turned out, it decided to go both ways.

During the Carboniferous period, there was only one continent on the planet. This land mass would be called Pangaea by scientists in later years. Yes, it is true that there was not always a North and South America tethered together by a thin Central America, or an Australia lurking down under, or a Europe, Asia, and Africa encircling a Mediterranean Sea like there is today. And Antarctica was not always a refrigerated zone of ice and snow and penguins. Such was the nature of this ever-changing planet Earth, as we have seen before, in which plates of rock shift around and climates transform over time. It would not be until the Cenozoic era's Miocene period when the land masses on the planet drifted enough and were knocked around so everything was rearranged into something similar to where the continents rest today.

I traipsed around Earth like I was in an enormous Triassic hands-on, high-adventure park. Some of the dinosaurs scared me greatly at first, but the fears diminished slightly when I gradually came to an understanding of their habits. I drove around in a mini jeep, previously stored in the space car tucked away somewhere in the corner of the basement. This useful vehicle proved to ride most excellently in all terrains.

I was able to photograph most of the dinosaur species. One of my favorite pictures was of me standing next to an ankylosaurus who was looking up directly into the camera setup. He had paused a moment from munching on his dinner feast of grass. Although I had a smile on my face in the photograph, the whole time I was a bit worried that the tank-like lizard might whack me with his strong clubbed tail. I was ready to spring away immediately if necessary. As it turned out, the wonderful monster was a real gentleman.

Wooly mammoths had the longest tusks I ever saw, with a markedly curved design. I envied these behemoths when the climate became cold, with their thick layer of shaggy hair up to a meter in length and fine underwool to keep them warm. On cold nights I often wished I would be capable of persuading one of these giant creatures to allow me to trim a few locks of hair so I might fabricate a robe that would keep me from freezing.

The first bird I saw was archaeopteryx, emerging around one-hundred fifty million years ago. This creature was very reptilian, and one thing I was certain about was I would not want it to visit any of my backyard bird feeders. Other flying animals were pterodactyls who, when they suddenly flew over me and cast their enormous shadows down, looked like fighter jets soaring high in the sky, seeking something upon which to pounce. Fortunately, they were never interested in devouring me, although on a few occasions they appeared to be interested in my cat, and I was successful in shooing these potential foes away.

It was sixty-five million years ago when a ten-to-twenty mile diameter asteroid hit the Yucatan Peninsula, causing seventy percent of the land species to go extinct. Fortunately I was able to jettison temporarily into space just before this occurred, having received an advance warning from my radar system. The dinosaurs were not so lucky, although the small mammals found a way to thrive afterward.

From these ashes the first primates arose. Then the apes arrived around thirty-eight million years ago, beating their chests and screeching loudly so the whole jungle could take notice. Twenty-five million years ago I often saw proconsuls sitting atop huge logs as if posing for a photograph, specifically like one of those early ones from the 1800s in which great-great-great-great-and-so-on great grandfathers and grandmothers appear in stoic pose. I did manage to get a few snapshots of these proconsuls, suitable for framing on the wall of any human's family room.

Around six to eight million years ago, I saw the chimpanzees go one way at the fork in the path while the hominins, which included prehumans and humans, took the other route. They were branching out with new abilities and desires. There was no turning back.

At least about one-hundred twenty-thousand years ago, Homo *sapiens sapiens*, the first modern humans, the actual species that still thrives today, first appeared on Earth. They were born in Africa, which had also been the breeding ground for all the related species that preceded them, such as Homo *habilis* and Homo *erectus*.

Because they were hunter-gatherers, each of these humans required a certain amount of acreage on which to live. As their population increased, they found it necessary to spread out. One male, irritated, explained, "We go out in the morning to pick berries, but find the Obabwe family already out there in full force, in the best fields, kneeling down or bending over with their butts high in the air, harvesting every berry in sight, leaving us with lesser fruits from which to pick. Not that we disliked them, but this happened one time too many for comfort and so we decided to relocate to a new place. We needed to move on."

These people were pioneers, venturing away from known lands to parts never before seen. "As we trekked away from our homeland, we had fears that we might be heading for disaster in some place very foreign to us," explained one thoughtful woman. Another added, "Yeah, and we never knew if there would be enough food for us."

"Or happiness," interjected the first woman, "We were very happy where we were. We could never be sure we would ever be again as happy."

Then around one-hundred thousand years ago, Homo *sapiens sapiens* migrated out of Africa into other continents. To relocate, they walked far and wide. In certain cases, crude boats or floating logs assisted them. Some locations, like the Bering Strait, were frozen over, allowing people to walk over water with safe passage to new worlds. By twenty-seven thousand years ago, Homo sapiens occupied just about every nook in the world that is currently inhabited except places like Bermuda, New Zealand, and some Pacific islands. Around twenty-thousand years ago, they endured the period of time in which the Ice Age was at its coldest. By twelve-thousand years ago there were about five to ten-million humans scattered throughout the world. This represented a fairly large population for that time, but tiny if compared to the nearly seven-billion people who live there today.

Around eleven-thousand years ago, a child in the Middle East carrying a container full of seeds dropped some contents on the ground. The adults expressed displeasure and told him to pick them up. "He set about to pick up the seeds," said a woman from that tribe, "but he was sloppy, not very thorough." He picked up most of the seeds, but left quite a few on the ground. Later when those seeds sprouted up, someone took note and began talking about it. People said to the child, "Look what you did," to which he had no inkling how to respond, not sure whether he was in trouble again. A discovery had been made. Seeds could be placed into the ground where they would grow into plants that made crops. Farming had been invented. It was the start of the Neolithic revolution. Wheat and barley became the chief farm crops there in the Middle East.

Then around nine-thousand years ago, observant humans living in southern China and continental Southeast Asia independently invented farming, and rice was their featured crop. And then around seven-thousand years ago, industrious humans in Central America independently discovered farming, and corn was their specialty. In time, farming was independently figured out in many other places as well.

Word of these discoveries spread slowly in this world that did not have newspapers, radios, or the internet. There were no transcontinental cables. The world was devoid of cell phones, walkie-talkies, YouTube, and Skype. *Time* magazine and *Sports Illustrated* did not exist. The *National Enquirer* tabloid was not in circulation.

And when news of this component of agriculture did arrive to other people, it was not always embraced. One tribe derisively chuckled at what they heard. They strongly preferred to remain a hunter-gatherer society. "Why would anyone want to take all the time to plant that stuff and hope that it grows when there's already enough food available all around you! All you have to do is just move around and look about a little to find it!" laughed their tribal elder.

Another group thought about it and at first thought it might be a good idea. But then people there realized farming would compel them to set up roots, something they were just not inclined to do. "Once a nomad, always a nomad," they chanted. "When I tire of looking at these mountains here, I move on. Don't want to be stuck in one place for too long!" explained one member of that tribe as he chewed on a long stalk of marsh grass.

A different clan that did warm to the idea tried planting seeds in a rocky, infertile plot of land, one that unbeknownst to them could not possibly yield a successful crop. They simply were not agriculturally experienced enough to be aware of that. Had they used the beautifully rich and ample soil adjacent to the loser rocky ground, they would have tasted success. They refused, however, to plant there because that turf was reserved for a certain beloved sport they played, something reminiscent of a crude golf game. After they kept their fingers crossed as well as their toes and the poor soil failed to produce crops, in their frustration they quit trying again.

One reluctant group changed its mind about farming when it heard that wheat could be used to brew beer. "At first, we didn't want anything to do with it, but when a neighboring tribe invited us over for drinks one evening, we became more interested. Now we have our own beer-making production."

Little by little, more and more humans adopted this new invention called farming. "With agriculture, there came an improvement in our food supply," explained one plump woman. "The men still hunted when they had the time, but we were able to have more diversified dinners than before."

Another person, with large rugged hands, said, "Because we had a surplus of food just about every year, we had a need for storage vessels, and so many of our people became heavily involved in the making of pottery."

"Yes, and also the surplus eventually led to increased trade with other societies. This led our people to become aware of many unique items produced by other people that now became available to us," added a tall skinny person with noticeably longer-than-normal fingers.

An elderly man who walked with a wobble claimed that "The population increased because of farming. Seen it myself with my own eyes. Farming settled us into a sedentary existence. Before, when we were nomadic, we could not afford the luxury of having many babies and children to take care of; not when you had to be completely mobile, ready to move at an instant. But now I could be several times a grandpa."

"But a disadvantage of farming . . ." explained his best friend, a hunchbacked woman with a high-pitched voice, " . . . a disadvantage of farming that I don't hear you talking about was that, as we settled down into a plot of land, and groups of increasing numbers of people were now closer together, epidemics of disease occurred. Some of these even wiped out entire clans. It was so unfair and unfortunate, is what I kept thinking over and over."

Agriculture was a form of symbiosis, or cooperation, between different species of plants and animals. Farming is one aspect of it, but another was the keeping of certain animals by humans for food, fur, skins, transportation, pulling plows, and other uses. Agriculture nudged some societies to grow large enough and act collectively in ways that qualified them to be deemed "cities." With populations usually of ten-thousand people or more, these isolated and scattered places called cities developed over great amounts of time throughout the world.

Within these cities, the development of new ideas and fresh discoveries accelerated. Said a local street sweeper: "When we figured out a way of melding copper and tin to form bronze, a new and improved metal became available for manufacturing weapons, tools, and artwork. Yes, it is true, it was not always that easy to find and harvest the tin, but sometimes it could be traded for with people who did have it in abundance."

Another technological development was the wheel. I myself am foggy on where it actually originated because I think at the time I became ill for an extended bit of duration and was not able to travel around the world daily as I had regularly been doing before. So, correct me if I am wrong, but I later surmised that this invention had been rolled in to the Middle East by nomads from central Asia. Anyway, regardless of from where it came, it, like so many other inventions, helped advance people as they figured out all kinds of practical applications for it.

It took about five-thousand years after the advent of agriculture for the first "civilization" to emerge. Civilization was just a more sophisticated level of human organization, one that went beyond the kinds that previously existed so that now there were distinct changes, in the form of upgrades. There now were even larger crop surpluses and population increases than before. There was a greater importance placed on cities as societies came to feel a greater dependence on these urban centers. There now were more formal political and legal setups, attempts at standardization of measurements, improved transportation systems, and the undertaking of bigger architectural projects. There was occupational specialization, writing, recordkeeping, and increased trade and use of currency. The first civilization was Sumer, along the Tigris and Euphrates Rivers in present-day Iraq. Soon after, civilizations would also arise in Egypt, Pakistan, China, and Mexico.

Of course every civilization differed in the degree to which it entertained these characteristics. Take writing, for example. Writing permitted the keeping of official records of transactions and historic events. There was cuneiform scratched into clay tablets. There was hieroglyphics written on papyrus. Some civilizations had only very primitive stabs at writing, while others developed highly sophisticated methods. Some civilizations had no writing at all. And even though a civilization may have developed writing, it is true that the majority of its citizens remained illiterate, and this was the case throughout history until more recent times.

And with these greater concentrations of humans came a demand for more formal political structures. "In my city," explained a city dweller from Egypt, "there was a real need for a small government to handle disputes. I remember the time my neighbor badly needed irrigation ditches dug from the river to his land to save his crops which had been suffering from water shortages. Since the ditches would traverse various independently-operated plots of land and many people would be affected by decisions made regarding this, leadership and standard rules were required."

In China, a ruddy-faced market worker with thick eyebrows explained, "Someone wanted to buy a pinch of spice from me. I give him a pinch of it. He said the pinch I give him is smaller than the pinch I give someone earlier and so he demands more. I said a pinch is a pinch, but then he becomes irate and says the earlier pinch is not the equal to the later pinch and so I yell out, 'Can someone help me give a pinch of spice so this man stops yelling?' And then in comes this guy with some newfangled contraption that he uses to measure a pinch so that a pinch always will equal a pinch and only a pinch, no less, no more." With more people and increased economic activity, standards had to be established.

The civilizations came and went. In time, the classical period in history arrived, when everything was ratcheted up several notches more than before. Classical civilizations arose in places like Persia, China, the Mediterranean, and India. These places created extensive and durable cultural systems that served as a glue that bound people in these societies more closely together. Later societies would look back on their achievements with awe and reverence.

Because I was able to witness the birth of the earth and its subsequent history, owing to my enhanced lifespan, I was in a unique and intimate position to appreciate the great spans of time involved for all this to occur. To someone who lives eighty years, the unfurling of time on such a large scale is something not easily grasped, as I said before. But it is helpful to at least try to immerse oneself in a more profound understanding of this.

One way to attempt this is to reduce history to a smaller scale. Some scholars have put it into a form whereby they condense it one billion times so that one year becomes the equivalent of one billion years. Using this scale, the universe was created about thirteen years ago and the earth formed four-and-a-half years ago. Seven months ago the first multi-celled organisms evolved and three weeks ago the dinosaurs were wiped out by the asteroid impact. Only three days ago the first hominins appeared, and fifty-three minutes ago the first Homo sapiens emerged. Five minutes ago farming arose. Three minutes ago we would find the first civilizations.

Using this condensed time scale, you may be better able to understand just how long it has been for me to not have anyone of a similar species around. That has been a story of supreme loneliness, as you can guess, but one I won't delve into. The most significant point to get out of this is just how little time humans have been around to figure into the overall history of Earth!

And so from the gas and dust remnants of expired stars coming together to assemble into large rock structures, one of which became the planet itself, to the filling of the oceans with water, to the first sparks of botanical life and subsequent greening of the barren landscape, to the welcoming of the animal kingdom's widely-diversified members, I was in attendance.

I was there to see the colorful spectacles, and hear the turnings and twistings and rock collisions and bird calls and lizard roars, and smell the greenery flowering and the animal scents, and taste the fruits that grew wild throughout this world.

And human history, from its inception through the first civilizations and subsequent classical societies and beyond, right up to the present, was filled with discoveries, inventions, exploration, construction projects, entertainment, and ideas about religion and politics. Empires shone brightly and then faded. New nations emerged. What can I say? Human history—it was a wild ride. A lot had happened. And humans had many trophies and certificates on their shelf of achievements. They had done many things.

They figured out how to use natural resources. They discovered how to control fire. They worked metals such as gold, copper, iron, and steel to make jewelry, weapons, and other things with which to build further. They felled trees to manufacture furniture, homes, baseball bats, and paper. They directed water to power steam engines and mills.

They built huts, shacks, tree houses, hot dog stands, dog kennels, pyramids, and skyscrapers. They constructed dugout canoes, papyrus boats, balsa wood rafts, paddleboats, catamarans, jet skis, cargo ships, tugboats, surfboards, cruise ships, and aircraft carriers. They manufactured biplanes, dirigibles, B-1 bombers, fighter jets, and the Sputnik, Vostok, Apollo Eleven, and Space Shuttle spacecrafts. They made the horse-and-buggy, bicycles, unicycles, motorcycles, automobiles, pickup trucks, eighteen-wheelers, segways, and the steam train. They built the Parthenon and the Pantheon, the Hanging Gardens of Babylon, the Coliseum, Hagia Sofia, the Playboy Mansion, and the Taj Mahal. They set up dirt paths, paved roads, multi-laned superhighways, yellow-bricked roads, bridges, canals, and railroad tracks that linked one side of a country with the other.

They invented bricks, clothing, cement, the plow, cigars, clothing, glass, the saddle, stirrups, gunpowder, windmills, the compass, the printing press, microscopes, telescopes, light bulbs, telephones, the flush toilet, thermometers, the stethoscope, the harpsichord, the electric guitar, the whoopee cushion, the safety pin, and the ballpoint pen.

They communicated with each other by developing a wide array of languages throughout the world. They related to each other through sign language, Morse code, smoke signals, flares, the Pony Express, initials carved on trees, foghorns, Braille, pamphlets, signs, monuments that commemorated key events, newspapers, magazines, cable network talk shows, email, Facebook, and Twitter.

They traded, bartered, and engaged in all kinds of commerce. They minted coins and printed paper money. They traded in gold. They fabricated credit and debit cards. They sold products over the internet. They begged for cash at the busy street corners or washed your car window while you waited at the red light so you would be compelled to give them a donation.

They entertained themselves with harvest festivals, Halloween parties, gladiatorial contests, gambling casinos, karaoke nights, afternoon teas, all-you-can-eat brunch buffets, wine tastings, standup comedy, listening to radio mystery dramas, reality TV, and sitcoms. They played pranks on one another, using gags like joy buzzers or water-squirting pocket pens. They enjoyed watching events at sports stadiums, movie theatres, horse racing tracks, Nascar dragways, and opera houses. They played sports and games like baseball, football (also called soccer), cricket, rugby, the Olmec game of ulama, chess, tiddly winks, Nintendo, X-Box, the Olympics, Candy Land, checkers, and bungee jumping.

They explored uncharted territories. They raced to the South pole on skiis. They sailed on the Mayflower. They also sailed across the Atlantic Ocean on the Nina and Pinta and Santa Maria, arriving at a place that up to that moment was unknown to the other half of the world. Both worlds had lived in isolation of each other for thousands of years. The voyage of those three vessels began the irreversible, sustained exchange between these two places. They explored the darkest and thickest jungles. They climbed the highest mountain "just because it's there!" They dove deeper and deeper into the depths of the oceans to see what they could find. They crawled into and bumped their heads on low-lying ceilings of caves. They investigated what was up in crazy old Uncle Elmer's attic so they could find what he's been hiding all these years. They flew into space high above the earth.

They leaped forward with various medical advances over the years. At first, they attempted to heal injuries and diseases through supernatural beliefs, but later began relying upon science. They adopted a medical ethical code. They sought to maintain bodily balance of four fluids: blood, yellow bile, black bile, and phlegm. They cut out bladder stones, but experienced a high mortality rate. They vivisected animals in their attempts to learn how the human body functioned. In 1543 a magnificently illustrated and accurate anatomy book was published. They placed increased importance in the performance of autopsies to decipher pathologies, targeting "the cries of the suffering organs." They came to understand completely that when Edward Jenner muttered something like "Alas! I hear the lowing of a cow! Perhaps now I can discover a cure for smallpox," that an improvement in human lives would be on its way soon after. They raised the level of surgery when they departed from the tradition that surgeons were noneducated artisans who simply did what the medical doctor directed. They developed standardized medical examinations. They paid more and more attention to microbiology in treating diseases. Despite having a patient drink liquor before an operation and strapping him down with thick leather belts, surgery still required six strong men to hold down the person as he screamed in torturous agony while the surgeon struggled to cut and stitch as fast as he could. When they discovered the anesthetic properties of nitrous oxide, ether, and chloroform, they began to make surgery much more successful and bearable. Despite the improvements in surgical technique, however, there seemed no way to lower the forty-five percent mortality rate, which was mostly caused by infection, until carbolic acid and other agents were used as a method of antisepsis. They learned to transplant organs. They got the word out about preventative medicine. And they developed hearing aids, eyeglasses, leg braces, knee replacements, dentures, and all kinds of pills to help keep themselves hobbling along, despite their disabilities, into the future.

They founded a wide variety of religions to bring some degree of order to unorganized life, to provide something to believe in, to help regulate behavior, to supply rituals that would strengthen beliefs and provide a means to communicate with the supernatural powers, and to help satisfy the universal need to get answers to the religious questions such as *Who or what created the world?* They buried, commemorated, cremated, and mummified the dead. They established Hinduism, Buddhism, Daoism, Confucianism, Christianity, Islam, Judaism, and so many other religious systems that could try to put some order into a chaotic world devoid of answers. They searched for universal values such as trust, loyalty, friendliness, kindness, and courtesy. Religion played a strong role in attempting to regulate behavior through internal control, which means self-regulation of individuals from within. Religion helped glue families and entire cultures together as they sought to live their lives by adhering to certain standards. And despite these attempts, for many people there always would remain grey areas, where uncertainties lingered.

They governed themselves by setting up various political systems to bring some degree of order to unorganized life, to help regulate behavior, to supply rituals that could strengthen the unity of the people, and to accomplish large tasks impossible for individuals to achieve alone. They formed monarchies, oligarchies, dictatorships, and democracies. They experimented with communism, theocracy, feudalism, and socialism. Through government, they attempted, often successfully for a time, to glue cultures together. From the external controls of decrees, laws, and punishments, they attempted to regulate human behavior from outside, as opposed to internal controls which tried to achieve this from within each individual. They tried to figure out how much freedom would be appropriate for the people to possess. They struggled to determine how much government's role should be in people's lives, how much freedom was appropriate. They remain standing, to this day, with unanswered questions and uncertainties about what is the best way to be governed.

They created art, which reflected back their experiences in life. They composed songs, ballads, blues, tango, rhumba, mambo, son, ska, merenge, rock and roll, symphonies, and operas. They composed a third symphony that was completely revolutionary in the history of the world, followed by more masterworks, topped off by a ninth symphony that left everyone spellbound and flummoxed because no one knew how anyone could possibly carry on from there. They authored the *Epic of Gilgamesh, the Iliad and the Odyssey, Great Expectations,* and *Madame Bovary.* Using red ochre mixed with water, they painted cave walls where the irregular rock surface, when illuminated by flickering torches, produced a sensation of movement in which animal figures seemed to come alive. They decorated the ceiling of the Sistine Chapel. They drew murals on city buildings and graffiti on subway walls. They opened tattoo parlors. They offered face painting at children's get-togethers. They produced sculptures of metal, wood, plaster, and stone.

They broke my heart. They figured out ways to slide the knife in and twist. They inflicted unimaginable atrocities upon one another. They designed instruments that could efficiently rip the fingernails from a person's hand. They used their imaginations to produce all kinds of implements of torture. They devised methods to kill one another. They found uses for knives, arrows, catapults, bombs, and missiles. They fought perennial wars over the centuries, incessantly rearranging the geopolitical boundaries on the maps. They practiced infanticide. They raped. They enslaved groups of people. They put their hands on automatic rifles and went into public gatherings to shoot as many people as they could. They poisoned the drinks that other humans would imbibe. They ripped off the skin and broke the balls of countless victims. The truly heinous acts they committed upon each other fills volumes, and scars our faces as tears descend hard in the rainfall. It wasn't enough that everyone already played on a harsh, rugged, precarious and often unforgiving landscape, but they went beyond that and took it upon themselves to ratchet up the pain, cruelty, and misery so it went farther than the horrors brought on by the natural physical forces here on this planet. Thank goodness for those moments of respite, the times of positive accomplishment and progress, the periods of peace and happiness that interrupted the chains of tragic events humans so often and regularly brought upon themselves.

*

And as I watched human history unfurl over the centuries, I came to an awareness of an unmistakable oneness. And although it was all well and good to say this oneness existed, I realized it was necessary to explain just exactly what it was and what you were to do with it. Over time I stumbled upon a road that could accomplish that.

Yes, all life and every inanimate thing on Earth arose from the same elementary particles, and there was a unifying, self-evident cohesiveness in that. All the atoms and molecules that came together to build the physical home had also discovered a way to recombine to form life, which then sprinted away, multiplying and evolving further. The same factory that produced rocks and dirt turned out cells, bones, organs, and the ability to sense environmental stimuli. It was all the same stuff. This was a physical oneness.

But there was so much more that brought it all together into a single entity. Things in this home were intertwined in more ways than one.

Every person who has ever lived is part of one big Human who builds and walks on a particular road. We could call this giant person "humanity" or "the Human."

The road represents knowledge. As humanity acquires more knowledge, a new segment of the road is laid down. The more the Human knows, the longer the road becomes. And pulled along with knowledge was the potential for wisdom and maturity.

The destination of the road is the Realm of Absolute Knowledge, the place where people would know everything. Here, all their questions would have answers. Does God exist? Who or what created the world? Where do you go when you die? Are there particles smaller than the tiniest ones we have currently identified? What exactly is in the center of the various planets? All questions have answers in the Realm of Absolute Knowledge.

It is a mark of maturity to accept the verdict that humans do not have answers to all the questions at this time. It is a distinction of honesty when people admit that they, as human beings, are limited in what they can currently know. Theoretically, the road may arrive at its destination some day, but for now, it has just not reached the Realm of Absolute Knowledge.

The road is a dirt path at its origin, later becoming a paved highway after humans improved their road-making ability. This road is suspended in space, with nothing above or below, and there is vegetation of all sorts, including grass and trees and bushes, on the hills and plains to the sides.

Look! There's the bougainvillea that used to grow with such vigor outside your apartment window in Havana! And there's the tall date palm that Queen Nefertiti once sat under while she gazed at the stars in the nighttime sky at Giza while listening to beautiful music played in the distance by a flute!

And if you look carefully, with a lot of patience, you can even see on and alongside the road the faces of every human who lived. You can look for everybody. It would be like trying to find Waldo—he most certainly is there, but you just have to search meticulously to find him because there's so many people. In fact, you can also see every animal that had ever dwelled on Earth if you look closely on the roadsides. All alive, and nothing run over by cars.

People who are alive today make up the active part of the Human, which is at the lead end of the road. People who are no longer alive make up the inactive portion of the Human and they trail behind on the road.

Beyond the most recently constructed edge of the road lies more empty space, but far in the distance can be seen the Realm of Absolute Knowledge. Humanity can continue to amass knowledge until it actually constructs enough road to reach that place where people would know everything. Realistically, it may never actually arrive there, although it certainly has the potential to get much closer to that place as the years pass into the future.

And after the dust settles, all of this is actually one entity—the road, the Human, the plants and animals, the physical home, the Realm of Absolute Knowledge. Everything that had a hand in the acquisition of knowledge is part of that road, thus the oneness.

Humans acquire knowledge by means such as observing, measuring, and testing. They learn by trial and error, by trying things to see what works and what does not. They also gain additional substantial knowledge by way of a learning process in which they build upon information that has already been established. I'll explain this further.

The philosopher of some early century—let's say Thales—goes through the motions of living his life, spending much of it thinking. As he manipulates ideas, he scratches his head and sweats profusely at times. He even falls into a well one day as he is walking and gazing upward, so deep in thought as he looks beyond the immediate to things of larger concern, not paying attention to his surroundings! But he recovers and writes down his ideas, concluding that "Water is the cause of reality." He pens many other thoughts, too, and his words are deemed original and important by the people reviewing them and so are given a place of high standing in the history of human knowledge.

Thales' ideas then become available to others, including the people of future generations, his words continuing to have significance when another philosopher—let's say Anaxagoras—enters the picture and reads them. Anaxagoras simply picks up the book and absorbs in a relatively short amount of time knowledge that took the first philosopher the great part of a lifetime of hard work to discover and organize. The second philosopher does not have to waste time starting from scratch grappling with those same ideas to the identical degree as did the first philosopher, who was a pioneer into that territory. He does not have to reinvent a wheel. Because of this economy of time, the second philosopher benefits by then altering or stretching the original ideas of the first philosopher. Anaxagoras develops his own conclusion that water is not the prime causer of all things but that something he calls "nous," or "the mind," is. The level of human knowledge is expanded.

You might question what is so important about designating water or nous as the primary causal agent of life. Well, these represent stepping stones that would grow over time into boulders as humans moved up on the ladder of learning.

Of course, this example of the growth process of learning includes the work of the great scientists, politicians, mathematicians, engineers, doctors, and brilliant individuals from the other professions as well. All contribute to new areas of knowledge, largely building upon what was learned before, while throwing in their own ingenuity. As they say, "We stand on the shoulders of giants."

It is important to also realize that not all the knowledge that is available today is absolute knowledge. After all, people have not yet arrived at the Realm of Absolute Knowledge. Because of their limitations on the road that they build, not all the scientific "facts" of today are actually absolute facts; much of what humans regard as true now will change to be in effect false in the future. Think of scientific "facts" that were considered true in the

1300's but yet, with passage of time, have been proven false. For example, the earth was once firmly believed to be flat, but that was eventually refuted. I remember cringing while I watched people defend the belief of a flat Earth as they engaged in fisticuffs. I just wanted to scream out that the planet was round!

Knowledge about the world constantly changes as humans learn more each day. The important thing is that the particular information that is regarded as being true—that is, knowledge arrived at via the best human capabilities available at the time and believed to be accurate—may perhaps not be *absolutely* true— but *relatively* true and usable for gaining "more correct" knowledge, enabling humans to move closer to the Realm of Absolute Knowledge. Humans build with present "truths," and in so doing, either find those to remain valid for now or in need of disposal as they are replaced by newer and "better" truths.

So I have pointed out that some prominent individuals are able to greatly influence humanity because of their ability to advance knowledge, based to some large degree upon their successful grasp of ideas laid down before their time, as they secure a place inside the encyclopedias, worthy of note. These brilliant people deserve praise and gratitude; as they absorb all the individual contributions of everybody else, they are able to go beyond what the average human being is capable of achieving. They have the capacity to assimilate the surrounding influences and then reflect these back in a meaningful way.

It must, however, be realized that this economical growth process by which people stand on the shoulders of these giants occurs not only with the great philosophers, scientists, politicians, and artists—it happens to you and every man and woman who has ever lived on Earth. In subtle ways, all the people of the present have gained something from every person of the present and past.

Take one of the first humans living on Earth, let's say a cave dweller, and understand that he acted and thought in certain unique ways, influencing the others who grew up around him. One hot, humid day, he influenced his friends when he smiled despite the fact that everyone was suffering from the heat as they worked hard in the sun gathering food. The smile was contagious and was never forgotten. It ignited their senses to form a lasting memory. People he influenced in this way then went on to do their parts in the daily activities of the society, each contributing happily to the growth in knowledge. Perhaps they would think of that smile in the future when the going got rough and they needed to smile. This they learned from that person.

In the instance that I just described, I wanted to take a seemingly insignificant trait and show it to be all-important, which it is indeed. Human beings gain the smallest things from each other. Every little action is soaked up in ways they often cannot even notice or comprehend.

I will next give a more readily apparent example of the knowledge-accumulating process by which common people influence each other. Despite the adverse conditions and the fact that everyone else had given up on the unsuccessful attempt to toil in the extreme heat to gather food, the cave dweller who kept smiling also devised an original plan which enabled the group to more swiftly and more comfortably accomplish their task. He devised a technique, a very specific method of shaking the branches a certain way so that the berries would fall off easily. He was able to rally the gatherers with his idea, which was then carried out successfully. The whole group increased its knowledge about food gathering, and would use this to their advantage later during future food-gathering sessions in times of extreme heat. So people learned a new technique from that cave dweller.

Let me expand this even further. That same individual also influenced other people simply by going through the motions of performing mundane chores at home or doing routine tasks while engaged in work. Let's say he labored as a farmer. His toils helped feed other people, who in turn contributed to the society's growth in knowledge.

Perhaps the food he harvested may have directly fed the guy or lady who invented a superior type of plow. Or it may have fed other people who associated with or assisted in some way that inventor, the cave dweller/farmer thus indirectly influencing the creation of this device.

So people were influenced by seemingly insignificant things like the cave dweller's smile, or by more apparent actions such as his food-gathering plan to beat the heat or his routine farm work. After the cave dweller died, the people he came in contact with during his life still possessed a part of him: his influences. His actions, no matter how small or seemingly insignificant, had influenced the people with which he interacted. Subconsciously or consciously, some of that caveman rubbed off on other people, which in turn passed to the next generation . . . and the next . . . and onward. In a sense, he is immortal because these influences continue to be handed down from generation to generation. The people of the present own a piece of him. They have an intimate connection with the people of the past. They carry a part of each person who came before them, whether they like it or not, despite the fact that many of them were real knuckleheads.

The common person, one not recognized by individual name in the history books, is thus very significant, for his actions and thoughts, no matter how small, affect every other person. These influences may be subtle or overt and occur at every moment of life. They influence world history. You don't have to be a celebrity to be significant. The small contributions of the common person add up to the success of the larger figures such as Mozart. Common people are members of the backstage crew providing support to the ones who are in the limelight. Overall, one may sense a binding relationship among people of the past, present, and future. People all have and will continue to affect each other, mostly in small ways that add up to larger influences. Maybe that is something similar to the way the earth itself was formed, as we saw before, where tiny particles become larger over long periods of time, where little processes add up to huge entities.

By performing whatever it is each person does at work in his or her occupation, and doing all the other things that do not have to do with work, big and small, in the course of each day, human beings build the road. All human activity contributes to the world's accumulation of knowledge.

The better, more efficiently, that these tasks are performed, the more effectively will humanity construct the road, building it much faster and closer to the place of absolute knowledge. Every road worker is significant in this endeavor, individual people acting like cells in a body, each with specific functions that are essential for the operation of the larger body. When a worker is ill or fails to show up for work, the rest suffer since advancement in road construction is hindered. If a person bangs his or her finger with a hammer, progress will be adversely affected.

And just as an individual person may grow through various stages in life, acquiring knowledge and progressing in wisdom and maturity, from infant to teenager to adult, so too does this Human, acquiring and applying knowledge as it builds a new extension of the road upon which it walks. If the Human was to act unwisely or immaturely, waging unnecessary violence, for example, the construction process could be delayed or part of the road could be damaged. A setback to the world's accumulated experience occurs.

The more violence people unleash among themselves, the less productive energy can be thrust into the pursuit of knowledge, wisdom, and construction of a better world. There will be more potholes in that road, thus hindering humanity's advancement toward the Realm. The children of that generation of people will occupy their own work time repairing the damage the parents have done, and this will detract from their progressing closer to the Realm. Imagine the damage to the road if a nuclear holocaust wiped out entire museums or rendered industrial how-to diagrams illegible. People are more efficient in the road building when they refrain from blowing up things and each other.

So this is the road I had stumbled upon, discovered only after eons of time had transpired. The road is a measure of the level of collective knowledge attained by humans and it includes everyone and everything that has had a hand in achieving (or detracting from) this level. Because of the interconnectivity, in the end it is therefore everything that exists. I attempted to explain how it is put together and how it works.

As I look back at it now, I can take a snapshot with my camera to capture the faces of all the bandaged, weary travelers trudging along on this working vacation, just carrying on as best they can. All these living things laughing, overeating, crying, stepping in poop, falling, running, rubbing against poison ivy, singing, dancing. Yes, I see giraffes, brush-tailed possums, raccoons, dogs and cats, people, and white birch and evergreen trees living atop a harsh, rugged, precarious and often unforgiving terrain, filled with an abundance of pain, cruelty, and misery, and beauty and love and kindness. I see this road wind its way across the universe. *I also now see my own footprints.*

FOUR

He had a heart of gold. He cared, cared about it all. And I knew it was a genuine concern and not just some façade to impress me or anyone else. He was different from most other people. He was a serious student, taciturn and humble, absolutely interested in learning as much as he could about everything. The elders who taught him recognized these qualities in him. They knew they were dealing with a unique individual.

You know, it's like if everyone in the world was in one room and couldn't leave and had to socialize within the confines of that single room, and you were serious about things and inquisitive and that led you, through a lot of hard work and passionate concern, to acquire a degree of knowledge and wisdom and appreciation that provided you a more comprehensive view of life from a high promontory. Not that this made you better than everybody else, but just more aware and fulfilled. And there were only perhaps two or three other persons in that room who were on the same plane of interest as you but you couldn't find them because it was so damned difficult to maneuver through the densely-packed crowd, so hard to squeeze your way across the room. This was the way it seemed to be to me. Trying to maneuver through the suffocating air that blanketed and comforted "normal," popular, the commonplace to get to those like-minded people was a continually elusive, frustrating struggle.

I was fortunate to know him and be his friend. I felt as if I was on the same page with him. While everyone else was living it up and sipping their cocktails inside that room (actually, occasionally not a bad idea!), we had somehow fortuitously bumped into each other and, in so doing, subsequently shared an elevated and more all-embracing experience about life in this world.

Right from the beginning of my earliest years cohabitating on the planet with the human species, I felt it best to remain separated from direct contact with people so as to give them what I felt would be appropriate space to make their own history, independent of a foreigner's influence. I was determined to be merely an observer from afar, and thanks to the high-tech equipment that accompanied me on this voyage was able to very effectively chronicle their lives without interposing.

In time, however, it became more realistic and inevitable that some paths would cross despite my best efforts at striving for separation. My strategy relaxed when I allowed a measured amount of limited direct contact to occur. I befriended very small groups of people in various parts of the world, staying only a short time in each place, eventually leaving and proceeding to a new land for want of avoiding over-familiarity and what I sometimes humorously thought would be perceived by historians as inappropriate meddling. Somehow I was able to maintain a fairly low profile among as few individuals as possible while dodging potentially dangerous predicaments or ruinous liaisons. And despite my avoidance of entangling commitments and such, I did, however, find myself touched by very many wonderful and decent human beings who were trustworthy and caring, and of whom I came to genuinely admire and embrace.

I remember relocating my spacecraft from an increasingly densely-populated Middle East to an isolated part of pre-agrarian South America where I touched down in the highlands and set up a new base of operations from where I could continue to swiftly traverse far and wide during the normal course of each day, to return to my quiet retreat when the routine tasks were completed.

I constructed a small wooden home using available natural resources. From the front porch the view of the surrounding jungle lowlands and distant hills was spectacular, a landscape exhibiting so much scenic variety as it changed continually depending on weather conditions and the amount of light available at different times of the day.

High up here the air was thick. Down below it was a thin air that I came to know during my unforgettable hikes deep inside the jungle where the rain forest cacophony of birds and frogs filled the tight spaces between and around the hanging vines and outstretched limbs of vegetation.

One day as I sat looking out over the plain, a young boy suddenly appeared from behind a tree. "Where did you come from?" I spoke aloud. Frightened, he turned and ran away. I tried to follow him by taking a few steps in his direction but quickly relented, deeming it a useless endeavor—he was too swift and nimble and I had already lost his trail.

I returned to my lawn chair and pondered. Having settled here some time ago, I had never once encountered humans, although I was quite aware of a village a three-days-long walk away. Was this an adventurous traveler from there seeking childhood treasures or fun? Could there be an offshoot of that village closer to where I was located?

The terrified countenance he flashed toward me as he fled seemed to indicate to me that I would never ever see him again. Surprisingly, about ten minutes later the boy returned! But this time he arrived with an adult man. They did not flee but gazed at me from behind a bush. My instincts told me they did not harbor ill designs. I held up my hand, waving as if to say "It is okay here, it is alright." After a short while, they cautiously emerged from the brush.

The boy appeared to be about eight years of age and the man perhaps thirty. They had dark complexions and black hair. The child was a miniature version of the man, strongly resembling him in appearance and mannerisms as well. Eventually they approached and we exchanged gestures designed to put each other at ease by reaffirming that neither of us intended any harm. Looking back now, indeed this was the beginning of what would become a great friendship. I would eventually figure out that the young man, Otabu, was the father of the boy, who was named Tomu, and they had been out hiking when they stumbled upon me quite unexpectedly.

Of course we could not speak in the same language and so had to rely on whatever other means we could scrape up to communicate. They marveled at the space car, especially its areas of smoothness. They asked for permission to touch its exterior and, after that was granted, proceeded to stroke its surface as if it were a dog. They moved slowly around the car, smiling and nodding to each other as if they had discovered something that verified cherished fairy tales they had shared. Their eyes widened upon arriving at sections of the fuselage that had received multiple dings from space rocks and so were now pockmarked and rough to the touch, like sandpaper.

When Tomu and Otabu first saw the cat, they both instantly knelt down as if in reverence to this fanged creature. When she suddenly yawned and they saw her teeth, they looked at each other, and seemed to be in agreement that this was some kind of moment of wonder to behold and relish. The cat just yawned again and rested her head back down as she curled up in a ball, not to be bothered by any more humans for want of a serene catnap.

Over the course of the next few weeks, Tomu and Otabu returned almost daily, visiting with me a while each time. As the days went on, I gradually taught them my language while they tried to teach theirs to me. Our ability to communicate with each other had improved to a large degree, although there remained much to learn.

"I have two sons and a daughter," I told them. "They were studious. When they were very young, all of them liked to collect rocks. I could still see the excitement on their faces as they gazed at a shiny piece of coal, holding it in their hands, viewing it from various angles. The youngest boy turned out to be the athlete in the family. He went on to play soccer (rather, our equivalent of your soccer) professionally and made a nice career of it. All three kids were personable and worked pretty hard. And of course each one of them could also be a handful at times, too." I described my hometown and elicited laughter from them when I reminisced about many of the funny colorful people who lived there and who hung out downtown around the main street. That cast of characters kept me, a shy girl, entertained most days.

In turn, Otabu and Tomu opened up to me, telling stories about what life was like in their semi-sedentary village. I learned of the sad occurrence of how Otabu had lost his spouse when she contracted a fatal illness two years ago. He and Tomu stoically enumerated the sequence of tragic events and I could feel their loss. Life was now harder for them. At least in some ways, with the assistance of the remaining extended family, they were blessed in their circumstances and could effectively carry on. Fortunately, their days could still be very fulfilling and enriched by the cherished memories of the good times they could carry with them forever. And they had support from the community.

One day I happened upon an idea. I said, "Tomu and Otabu, can you bring your family here in a week from today so I can meet them? I will provide food and drink and we could all be together. I shall like to greet and hug each member of your family." At first, they looked at me with a hesitant, confused look as if what I said made not much sense. Tomu looked at his father, who paused and procrastinated but then smiled and accepted the invitation. We discussed matters a bit more, and then father and son were eager to return home so they could make preparations.

Over the course of the following week, I got things together and planned for the upcoming get-together. Tomu stopped by to assure me that everyone would be coming. The weather was looking favorable.

The morning of the feast I was awakened by snorting and the clanging of what sounded like cowbells. Lifting myself out of bed, I rubbed my eyes, yawned, and staggered half-asleep over to the window. I could not believe what I saw—there were hundreds and hundreds of alpacas and llamas assembled all around my house, stretching down into the spacious fields on either side for as far as the eye could see. There was also a substantial herd of cattle, along with various dogs and perhaps fifty people of all ages, young and old, camped out in my "yard."

"Oh, good God," I gasped aloud to myself as I abruptly realized my mistake, slapping my forehead and rubbing further my eyes to wake myself up. It now belatedly occurred to me that I had used the wrong word. Something got lost in the translation. When I issued the invitation, my intent was to invite the immediate family and to this end I used the native word, tigor, but now realized I should've said tig*ur*. Tigor, in their language, is some kind of superword that means the entire extended family plus all the friends, neighbors, coworkers, and animals associated with them. So that is how it came to be that I now had a rather large group of people and other assorted living creatures assembled outside my house looking for a party.

I emerged from my dwelling and had to honor my original proposition and so hugged every person and beast that had come to visit me. About two hours later, I carefully articulated, using an exorbitant amount of caution, through Otabu painstakingly verifying and translating (I wasn't going to take any more chances that I might slip and say something inappropriate that might invite further disaster) that it was a pleasure having everyone here and I offered whatever food and drink I had. They laughed and looked at each other as if to corroborate that "we knew she could not possibly have provided for all of us—tigor— without having the advantage of extra help." In their healthy skepticism, they had planned ahead, fortunately, and brought their own food to be added to whatever I supplied. They were understanding and accommodating, and the feast turned out to be a lot of fun.

They were curious about the space car, but seemed afraid to touch it. They were always sure to remain a certain minimum distance away from it. They respected me as if I was some kind of a god.

At the end of the day, the elders delegated the less than desirable job of picking up all the mounds of fresh animal waste to the youngsters, who worked efficiently without one complaint, although I had managed to see a most disagreeable expression on the faces of a young boy and girl as they gathered around one particularly large mound of droppings and prepared to pick it up.

In time, everyone gathered their wares and thanked me a million times, bestowing great affection upon me. It took quite a while to say goodbye to everyone and I was certainly exhausted at the end of the day.

After my guests departed and returned to their homes I occasionally saw more of the young people wandering up to say hello. And Otabu, too, visited often and became a trusted friend. As I had started a little farm on a small plot of flat earth, I would quite often be found tending to it. They expressed great interest in what I was up to. Eventually Otabu offered to help operate the farm. He could enlist the aid of hardworking individuals from his village. He and I could manage the farm's activities. I could not refuse, and so agreed to allow workers from the village to live and work on the farm.

We planted potatoes and coffee in large amounts, and other crops in much lesser quantities.

"Crops are really shining," Otabu declared one day to me.

"This is true. They grow very well indeed!" I responded proudly.

Otabu's people would be considered semi-sedentary foragers who were just getting into the incipient stages of agriculture. The farming part of it was very new to them and so they learned quite a bit from me. I should also say, however, that I too gleaned very much from the experience since I had never farmed at all during my years back on my homeland planet. Together we figured out many problems and ended up doing pretty well yielding successful crops.

Apart from the farm, I had been thinking a lot about the "oneness." Various ideas gradually developed and circumnavigated around in my head. What do you do with this awareness of oneness? What were its practical implications? It lucidly stood before me so I could never see anything anymore without that omnipresent sameness infiltrating everything it touched. How do you play with a singleness of identity, with this consciousness of homogeneity? That is what held my curiosity mostly.

I discovered Otabu to be a most thoughtful soul and began sharing with him measured descriptions of what I was thinking. He was an intelligent and creative man, who stood apart from his peers in his level of wisdom.

He was extremely receptive and genuine, a most admired and respected individual in my eyes, and the world's, for that matter.

We talked about the road. He knew what I meant by it. Otabu preferred to think of the road as a simple dirt path that was cleared further as more knowledge was gained. He had never seen actual roads paved over with flat stones or in widely cleared configurations. But the same principles applied. It was true that in the end we understood the same thing.

I asked him, "But why would we want to unselfishly work so hard to build this particular road as efficiently as possible? Why participate when no one knows if any reward like a heaven actually awaits our arrival some day? Why be excited and anxious to pitch in? Why assume such high-minded responsibility to each other? Why not just go it alone, every man for himself? Every woman for herself?"

He listened carefully.

I continued defining my burning question. "After all, there will always be individuals who would choose not to support the building of this road, for whatever reasons. They would openly reject many or all aspects of it. Some of them might gladly render intentional divots in this road as they go forth tearing up the night, wreaking havoc, raping and pillaging, and burning down the village. Or if not utterly destroying things, in more subtle ways they, through selfishness, a hyper-relentless pursuit of wants, an unwillingness to embrace camaraderie, or perhaps through some other related fault may, sometimes unknowingly, contribute to a detraction from progress in the road construction."

He answered solemnly, "Yes, yes. Beyond the obvious fact that we humans are naturally curious and want to know answers (some going to greater lengths than others of course!), want to increase our level of knowledge, I submit to you that perhaps we would desire to work as hard and effectively as possible to build the road simply because *we are all stuck in the same boat here on Earth*, not knowing answers to the most profound questions about life, surrounded by incessant dangers, just struggling to survive. We are so fragile here. This condition represents a common ground upon which we stand. As long as this is the landscape upon which we must dwell, this alone is an inducement to come together to learn more about this environment, for our own benefit. Out of a necessity to make things better, we are tied to one another. Because we are all in the same predicament, why not make the best out of a precarious situation?"

Yes, he described it as I believed it to be. And although perhaps many individuals would give much more noble reasons than this for assisting in the road's construction,

I told him that I thought this seemed to be at least a realistic bottom-line common denominator that most everyone could find a way to embrace.

You see, it is common sense that the more we learn about the world, the better we can make our living conditions. When we increase our knowledge about medicine, we are more capable of relieving pain and suffering from illness or injury. It angers me when I see innocent children have to battle leukemia, or hard-working adults in the prime of their lives become afflicted with muscular dystrophy or cancer. Is it fair to be struck down like this while you are just trying to live? When we come to know more about the weather, the more capable we will be to take precautions in advance of a hurricane's arrival so we might minimize the upcoming damage. When we try harder to figure out our interpersonal relationships, we can hopefully get along better with each other, again creating improved living conditions for everyone. The more knowledge in all aspects of life that we grasp firmly, the better. The knowledge we accumulate could serve in multiple practical applications to assist us as we proceed through our harsh lives on this planet.

"And of course," I added, " the less destruction we humans bring upon ourselves, the greater the progress on the road."

"Yes, yes," he began, "Unfortunately, the violence we inflict on each other has been a steady companion all along the way, as I am told through the stories we tell each other which get handed down from one generation to the next, and as I have seen with my own eyes."

"But despite the sometimes grim picture of destruction through natural as well as humanly-provoked misfortunes I have painted in our conversations over time, I possess eternal optimism," I declared.

Otabu quickly added, "Of course. There are a lot of bad things and unfair circumstances on this crazy planet, but when asked if the glass is half-empty or half-full, I neither respond idealistically that it is half full, nor do I respond pessimistically that it is half-empty. I respond realistically that it is both—half-empty and half-full."

"That's an honest answer," I responded.

"I am constantly aware of the negative as well as the positive in the world. I celebrate all the good, keeping an optimistic attitude, while never forgetting the bad things that I would continually work to eradicate or at least minimalize. It is my choice to believe that despite all that is unpleasant and injurious out there, there is always hope that those things can be defeated if we work hard enough."

"So," I inserted, "we have to have a little faith—choose to believe the world is an overall positive place that has negatives, but negatives that can be surmounted."

Otabu answered, "Yes, yes, I am with you most tightly with that."

I asked him, "And now, so, more specifically, what exactly can we do to work as hard and as efficiently as possible to build this road? In simple words, what's the best way to build the road?"

He thought awhile, then answered, "Yes, yes. First of all, we can each do the best we can building the road if we understand and accept this oneness, and then place an *awareness* of it in the forefront of everything we do each day so it *serves as a guide on how to carry on*, thus giving us a purpose and sense of genuine camaraderie as we recognize something that unites us with our fellow inhabitants and everything else in the world, promoting progress on the road. This is the deepest, most significant value to be found in the oneness, I think."

I enthusiastically answered, smiling widely, "I believe so, too! We are on to something here!"

At that moment, we were interrupted by several villagers who wanted us to watch their new dance and so of course we dropped our discussion and allowed our lofty thoughts to dissipate into the spacious sky above us for the time being while we got lost instead in the frolic provided by our friends down here on the ground. We laughed as we viewed the happy entertainment. Some of the youth began handing out cups and pouring cold water to anyone in the impromptu audience desiring a refreshing drink. Several of the older folks just smiled and respectfully watched the show.

The days passed and there was an absence of rain and the dirt trails became dry so dust was stirred into the air when people walked by. The colorful jungle animals screeched and cackled vociferously and the omnipresent insects whirled and darted all over and under the air around the village.

A few weeks later as I was peeling a mamey-like fruit, Otabu came running down the path excitedly calling out my name. The sun was beating down on us with its golden hot rays. There was a noticeable absence of even any hint of a breeze.

"I have something to add," he said. When he at last caught his breath, he declared, "There is something else I can add. Another thing we could do to work as hard and as efficiently as possible to build this road is to *achieve*! That is, *to push ourselves to be all that we can*!"

My face lit up in a smile. I was so blessed to have a friend like him who actually cared about these matters and who obviously had been struggling at attempting to discover more to add to our previous discussion! It was a wonderful thing to have people with similar passions put their heads together.

He continued, "Yes, yes, each one of us—every one of us—should be as physically and mentally productive as possible."

Then he laughed and added, " . . . unlike my brother-in-law, who as we know is not so motivated!"

In defense of his brother-in-law, I laughed and said, "But he was the one who rescued the kite from high up in that tree when it had blown onto the branches. The children flying it were crying and devastated, thinking they would never get it back. And no one of the adults was willing to climb so high . . . except your brother-in-law! Remember how he sweated and got scratched and retrieved the wayward kite?"

"Okay, yes. He was a hero that day . . ." responded Otabu.

"Indeed he was!"

"Yes, yes. But back to my point. It is good for us to be physically and mentally productive. This means for each of us to pursue our personal goals and develop our own unique abilities and talents to the fullest; to keep ourselves physically strong and healthy; and to aim to be mentally sharp so that we strive continually to be as educated and informed as possible. These personal achievements propel the road forward as we directly and indirectly contribute to the collective advancement of everyone else involved in the road construction."

I nodded and touched his shoulder, cautioning that "I think you got something there, but doesn't that sound a bit self-serving?"

"Well, as I just said, our personal achievements contribute to the collective advancement of everyone else involved in the road construction. But in addition, the beautiful thing is that when we be all we can be and thus take care of ourselves, we are then better capable of directly taking care of others as well; we simultaneously hold ourselves available to assist others when they need a boost. We need to carry each other from time to time. When we strive to keep ourselves in top physical condition, for example, we do so not just for our own benefit but to be an asset to the rest of the world. If a building catches fire and a person is injured to the point where self-evacuation is not possible, it would be to that person's advantage if we were strong and healthy enough to carry that person out rather than be unable to accomplish that rescue due to our being in poor health."

My craving to elaborate and further develop practical applications to this road and its world of oneness seemed to be carried along now to a greater extent than ever, thanks in part to my friend Otabu.

Several months later I haplessly realized the shrinking effect I described earlier, that scientific unexplainable glitch that would descend upon me, was about to begin and would arrive with a rapid and forceful surge. I knew my body and it was telling me something new was happening. Through the use of my medical equipment I was able to confirm what was to come. I still had perhaps about a month or so before it would commence and during this time agonized about what to do about it.

With much remorse, I decided it best to say goodbye to my wonderful friends before they could witness me transform into someone who could no longer communicate with them. A sad cloud had formed around me. I simply told them I needed to depart, without going into specifics. They trusted me so much that they did not attempt to pry more of an explanation from me, except for Otabu, who felt so dejected that he was inclined to beg me for more of an explanation.

One of the last nights together, Otabu and I sat around a campfire that helped warm the chill in the air. We talked about "old times" in our relatively short time together on this earth.

He said, "Do you remember when you caught the fish with the net Tomu made and hoisted it up onto the land but it kept flipping so much and so vigorously that it leapt up and slapped you in the face pretty badly only to escape by launching itself off your forehead so that it was propelled back into the water?" He laughed so hard, as did I too. He was right—that was certainly a hilarious moment.

In turn, I recalled the day Otabu scratched his leg severely on a large thorny plant he had fallen into. The local healing method of wrapping the injured skin in a particular leaf did not seem to work to heal it like it normally should have. I went into my medical kit aboard the space car and applied a certain greasy yellow ointment which immediately altered the situation for the better. Within three days, Otabu's injury was healed and word of this "miracle" spread throughout the settlement. Otabu said, "I am forever grateful."

Otabu had more on his mind that he wanted to share with me. He began, "There is something else, one thing additional, an idea that grows it and then tops it all off. Yes, yes. There is one more thing we can do to build the road as effectively as possible: it is to *respect*. Yes, yes. That is, it is to inundate our lives with a profound sense of genuine respect toward everything on the road, regardless of which directions we are blown around in as we wind our way through the jagged, twisted corridors of daily life. After all, everything else is part of us anyway. The way we treat all else comes to be the same as being the way we behave toward ourselves."

"Yes, I hear what you are saying. That one word is like the glue that would hold it all together."

Otabu continued. "If I respect you, I would not lie to you. If I respect you, I would not cheat you. If I respect you, I would not mislead you. If I pass along information that is not true, I deny you the ability in turn to make good choices since your decisions would be based on the disreputable message I provided you with. How can the road be effectively built if this is the way it would be? If I respect you, I would not for my own selfish convenience casually dispose of moral principles that happen to be in the way of things I want. And if I respect my children, I would not neglect them by spending, at their expense, excessive time pursuing my own selfish hyper-relentless pursuit of things I desire. If I respect you, I would certainly not steal from you nor commit any violent crime against you. To do these terrible things to other people, we would have to relinquish any sense of respect toward the ones we offend.

When we respect others, we treat them with fairness, the way we ourselves would like to be treated. It is fair when I am careful to consider how my actions affect other individuals. We know that it is fair when we take pains to allow others an equitable chance to pursue their goals. It is fair when we desire that others attain their own aspirations too and our actions are carefully undertaken to allow this. It is unfair whenever we pursue things we want in an unfettered, relentless way, without restraint, often at the expense of other people who play by the rules. When things are not fair, people are denied the chance to pitch in their talents, and so overall progress on the road is obstructed."

"But," I interrupted, "it is all well and good if you approach all things in life with this great level of respect, but what happens when those whom you approach do not treat you with respect?"

He answered, "Those are the grey areas of conflict. Those are the places where atrocities arise. I believe you must carefully consider each episode as it comes up. What I am trying to say is to be realistic, but nevertheless utilize a more profound sense of respect than we are accustomed to; give others a chance and in time determine if they are returning the respect you give out. And that is another story! Let's talk about that some time!"

Then, after we both paused silently for a few minutes, I returned to the matter of respect being the glue that holds things together. I proceeded, "I would venture, moreover, when we uphold a sense of respect, we direct it not just at other people but also toward everything else that is in this world, when we acknowledge how all is linked and that there is a beautiful, complicated, and delicate balance of nature that exists, where an action in one place causes an effect somewhere else, and we act appropriately and responsibly always with this awareness in mind. It is with awe that we may think of fish surviving miles below the ocean's surface in pitch dark, of the interplay between atoms in organic chemical reactions, and of all the other amazing things in the universe. If we approach these in a respectful way, we build the road better."

"Yes, yes," Otabu said, "I don't know what you mean by things like 'atoms,' but I do know nature is like a beautiful piece of dynamic, ever-changing art that I view with awe. The accomplishment of a Creator, whether the creator is a person, thing, or some force we cannot yet make out, is no small task. I respect this Artist's world as I strive to understand it better so our living conditions might improve. As we build the road, we can move forward with respect as we try harder to understand these interactions and apply knowledge more wisely to help our situation while avoiding detrimental effects to fellow inhabitants of the planet and the balance of nature. The more we learn, the better it would be for all things and for all life here."

Otabu could not have said it any better.

And so I have told you, as best I could, what I found out.

People participate in rituals to remind them about and reinforce their beliefs so they would act more consistently within a desired framework. Prayer—an attitude adjustment, really—is one form of ritual and if I were to enter into the quiet reflection of prayer in the form of thinking about the people of the world and my wish for them to be healthy, safe, and happy; when I mentally reviewed how well I had lived and how I could strive to do better still; when I reaffirmed my genuine team mission and desire to maintain a true camaraderie with everyone else; when I thus, all in all, contemplated the oneness of everything . . . and this inspired me to go out into the daily shuffle with renewed determination, ready to confront the world with fresh energy and confidence . . . and I carried this with me throughout every moment of each day as if I was enveloped in a kind of perpetual prayer . . . it would be then that I would be holding high the lantern of oneness so everything ahead of me was inundated with this brilliant light of cohesiveness influencing everything I did, from the most trivial to the more tangled-web complex, so that I would be completely in tune with everything that surrounded me. I then affect local situations favorably which then transmigrates to more remote places, ultimately touching the rest of the world. Waves of influences are sent throughout the planet, positively stimulating it. In our own little ways, we move mountains.

When we arise in the morning, do we feel a sense of unity with others? And with the entire world? A sense of common purpose—that what I plan to do in the upcoming day is going to mesh in some way with everyone else's plans to collectively produce a positive achievement? Do you wish you had a sense of higher purpose, giving you some meaningful link with other people and everything that exists in the world?

I realize it is not possible to directly love and embrace people who live halfway across the globe, people I have never met. For that matter, I realize it is not feasible to smile and say hello to every single person that passes by me on a busy city street. We do, however, touch them in indirect ways by respecting and loving the people who are closest to us in our lives. We thus send waves of influences that affect the people near us, who in turn touch others, and so on it goes. By taking care to nurture our immediate relationships, the relationships which have the most meaning to us, we indirectly spread our love and respect throughout the world. By concentrating on living in the best way possible on a local level, acting with good moral character and respecting life and developing our aptitudes to our fullest abilities and so on, we touch the rest of the world. As the saying goes, "Think globally, but act locally."

And so I came to live with an awareness of oneness that I held in the forefront, working hard and efficiently as possible to develop my aptitudes and talents to the fullest with fairness and a genuine spirit of camaraderie and respect to build the road and thus contribute to the collective act of increasing knowledge so that the road gets closer to its destination, producing improved living conditions. This was the right way to carry on here.

Imagine the youth getting all this down from us. There would be less uncertainty and more confidence in their lives, both when they are young and later when they are old. Imagine if our kids got all this from us, so much so that they could be found wearing it imprinted on their cool, hip T-shirts or so that they could be overheard laying it out in their casual discussions amongst themselves. Imagine them embracing the oneness and turning, turning toward a life enveloped with a spirit as exemplified by those rare few souls who every once in a while come along and give of themselves so wholeheartedly that others less fortunate than they could feel some respite from the cold hostilities surrounding them. Imagine compassion and respect loitering about like never before, so that there were more people like the Mother Teresa who wore the same garments of the sick whom she served with her whole heart and soul, sacrificing endlessly since she realized it was not possible for her to be happy and content when there were others out there who could not even find food to eat or bandages to dress their wounds.

Imagine a world where every driver was concerned to avoid running over the smallest of animals who dart across the road; where every human would not ever think of packing chickens in cages so closely together that there could be no turning around; where you would never cut down a tree without first giving wildlife a chance to relocate their nests under conditions favorable to them. Imagine all these little things that we are presently inclined to shrug off as insignificant becoming the standard of care.

I feel an immense responsibility to the people of the future. They will someday inherit the road from us. The collective integration of our current branches of knowledge allows the realization that the mind is limited in its ownership of the Realm of Absolute Knowledge. The world of the Unknown Artist elicits an infinitude of inquiry and, I unselfishly admit, it is our children who will further our possession of fact; the limits of their ability to accomplish this depends upon what we do today. As for now, I embrace the beauty of this masterpiece, cuddling a wealth of happiness from the enthusiastic awareness of its goodness and being . . . and I realize I too am an integral part of its mysterious scheme. I walk with care and respect around the dangerous parts of the landscape, and if only a universal respect for this artistry would blossom, I am sure that elusive peace and maturity would settle as a loyal and adherent companion of life. Just imagine.

Perhaps our most important purpose is to unselfishly work as efficiently as possible to prepare the way for the people who will live here after we die. When we leave this world, a part of ourselves always continues on in all the other people and things we touched with our life, and so we are immortal in that way. As our children travel closer to the Realm, we, in death, go with them.

After that evening around the campfire, I made the necessary preparations to leave my friends in South America. With profound sadness, I bid farewell to each of them. To Otabu I obviously could not give a routine farewell. It was one of the most difficult things I ever had to do. He begged me to stay but I explained why I could not. After the dust settled, he trusted me and realized I had to do what I had to do.

He said, "Then, as I remain here, separated from you, know that, despite the distance, where you go, I go. And where I go, you go too. Because there is that which we shared and it is good forever. Remember that always."

Full of tears, our discussions left unfinished, I nodded, "I know."

I entered the space car and lifted off, deserting the land of a thousand alpacas. I traveled somewhere far away and within the next two weeks was enveloped by the predicted devolution in mass. Not only was I stuck on Earth and without ability to communicate with my own planet or return to it, but now I could no longer interact with the humans. So I now had to adapt to these new circumstances. I was able, however, to continue to observe and record all that happened on Earth, hoping that perhaps the memoir and film footage might one day be able to help those whom I deeply considered to be my brothers and sisters.

FIVE

Rabbits sometimes skipped across the small backyard lawn of Harry Smirkowsky's home in Pennsylvania. Today, a beautiful summer day in July, a brown cottontail scurried, stopped abruptly, looked around, then hopped relaxedly toward the unpainted wood fence that separated Harry's land from that of his neighbor's. Abutting the fence was a carefully stacked pile of downed tree branches and logs that served as a comfortable shelter for rabbits and chipmunks. The brown rabbit joined a fluffy white companion and they both disappeared under the heap.

A row of tall green hedges on the opposite side of the yard served as a boundary with other neighbors—a man and woman and their eleven children. A single-car garage formed the rear demarcation, along with another, unmatching, fence that separated Harry's property from a third neighbor, an old man who tended to his pigeons and kept mostly to himself.

Brightly-colored flowers were planted in a rather spacious garden near the back door of Harry's house, with blues and yellows and reds and whites organized creatively in round groupings, each the diameter of a Mack truck tire. Bees visited the floral arrangement, carrying on productively with their daily routines.

Harry and Ann were married twenty years and had three children, of which the oldest, Stephen, was fifteen, followed by Mark, ten, and Gregory, eight. For many years, Ann's parents lived with them, until they passed away within one month of each other two years ago.

White birch trees grew well in one corner of Harry's yard. A tall cherry tree produced fruit regularly in another nook. At six-foot four in height, Harry was tall enough to pluck cherries from their branches whenever he wanted. Both husband and wife worked hard to keep this property neat, with a well-trimmed lawn and manicured hedges. This place was their sanctuary where they came as often as they could to sit and reflect or entertain friends.

Harry's children liked to crawl down the rock wall on the side of the hedges, descending to the yard of the neighbors who had the eleven kids, whose backyard had a grapevine and a broken patio. It also had a large rectangular patch of dirt, level at one end but framed with a tall dirt pile at the other, a perfect playground for young kids. Harry's youngsters kept their Tonka toy construction trucks there at all times along with the neighbors' model tractors and bulldozers, ready to be engaged to move the dirt around. The children spent countless hours there building mountains and valleys with patted-down roads on which the vehicles could roll their wheels. They caught earthworms and watched them wriggle back into the soil. Sometimes they flowed water from the crimped and rotted black garden hose into low-lying cuts in the ground to simulate rivers and streams. They played with toy soldiers in mock battles, the enemies made to engage on the solid plateau they had carefully erected.

They also had miniature plastic dinosaurs and on some days would set them up among the various surface irregularities of the dirt landscape, adding a rock here or there and leaves and clumps of moss to complete the prehistoric terrain. One of their friends once came over from another part of town and erected a volcano that came in a science kit he received as a gift the previous Christmas. This demonstration was a hit with all the kids.

Jason, one of the neighbor's eleven children, said "The brontosaurus makes loud noises when it walks because it's so heavy." He proceeded to stomp the fake dinosaur's feet into one of the roads his friends had built, continuing to pound the ground. Jimmy cried out, "You're making an earthquake!" The playmates then pretended there was a giant earthquake as they rigorously dismantled the miniature landscape. It would get rebuilt the next day by the toy construction trucks, of which there was every kind you could imagine, ready to haul and spread rocks and dirt.

While the children played in the dirt, Harry and Ann enjoyed chatting in the quiet of their backyard, sipping lemonade on this warm summer day. Ann had just prepared the drinks in her brightly-decorated modern kitchen. The radio on the tabletop was on, softly playing the blues that emanated from a particular local station specializing in that type of music.

Joe, the father of the eleven children, yelled from the rock wall to Harry and Ann. They saw his face peering up at them through a clearing in the hedges. He asked if they saw the recently-discovered surface vein of coal that was now perpetually burning near their homes. The old anthracite mines, lying idle among the quaking aspen and birch trees and ferns, and the ignited coal were located in the woods across the street.

Near the mines, the neighborhood children enjoyed playing baseball in a flat, open clearing atop ground that had been littered with rocks and pebbles. The kids, upon the urging of Joe, had pitched in together to remove as many rocks as possible. They brought rakes from their families' garages and ended up doing a fine job clearing the ground and smoothing the surface so that it now served well as a makeshift sports field. They also leveled off any surface irregularities that marred the landscape.

Joe said the coal fire was a bit deeper in the woods, just beyond the field, along the edge of the old culm dump where the unwanted silt and slate was piled up after the valuable coal was transported away for processing. Some coal, however, was left behind as was inevitable, and now had ignited and spread to the surface vein. These things happened from time to time in coal country. This incident was of a small scale and not posing any major threats, assured Joe.

Harry said, "We've walked over there when it gets dark out to see the burning rocks glowing red and blue."

"If you get close enough to it, you can hear the crackling sounds," added Ann, dressed casually in a floral blouse and old worn slacks.

Joe, wearing his New York Yankee ball cap oriented atop his head with the brim to the rear, said, "Even from here, there is a sulfur smell filling the surrounding air."

Then Harry reassured, "There's no plants or litter too close to the coals for anyone to be concerned about any spreading of the fire."

Harry's fifteen-year old son entered the yard as the adults conversed, dropped off by an older friend who drove a gas-guzzling pickup truck that needed obvious muffler work as it belched black smoke. Harry's neighbor couldn't help but notice the tee shirt Stephen was wearing, which had "Proud to be African-American" printed on the front.

"Now tell me, Harry, what's that supposed to be all about? Your boy is as white as Frosty the Snowman . . ."

"I don't know. I tried to tell him his grandparents were from Poland and Ireland. You'll have to ask him about it. I told him he probably should get rid of the shirt. But I don't know. He's a smart kid."

"These kids these days! They come up with a lot of silly ideas!" retorted the neighbor, trying to suppress his overall disgust with the matter.

When Stephen came up to the front porch and said hello, the neighbor stubbornly decided to pursue the issue further, and asked, "What's up with the shirt?"

The boy appeared to be in a hurry as he darted by, quickly explaining as he strode into the house, "Don't you know we all have origins in Africa—that's where the species began and then spread throughout the rest of the world. So you and I are just as African-American as Michael Jackson, Mr. Custer. And our predecessors had kids who played just like today's children. And the adults back then faced struggles to survive, just like now."

As the front door closed, the neighbor murmured something about the schools putting bad ideas into the kids, "throwing everything topsy-turvy."

Harry just looked blankly into the distance, then chuckled to himself without saying anything. Joe excused himself, saying "Gotta' go, you guys. Have a good one."

"Yeah, get outta' here! We're Mets fans in this house anyway!" yelled Harry. Joe cracked a smile as he exited Harry's yard.

Harry was a coal miner just like his dad and grandfather. He was trying to rest up in preparation for his next work shift.

It took millions of years for the earth's supply of coal to form, most of it arising from plants such as trees and ferns that lived between two-hundred fifty and four-hundred million years ago in vast swampy forests. After these plants died and collapsed into the water and sunk to the ground, they began to decay, but only rotted partially because of the lack of oxygen in the swamp water. As more plants died over great stretches of time, a thick layer of partially decayed downed flora accumulated, forming a soft, brown material called peat.

Later, the weight of dirt and rocks that had come to cover over this accumulation pressed the water out of the peat and increased the temperature. The heat and pressure hardened the peat into the sedimentary rock called lignite, a brown kind of coal.

As even more layers of sediment were eventually deposited, the heat and pressure increased so much more that the lignite changed into bituminous coal, a soft, black type of coal. Then, with even more surface deposition, the forces were magnified and anthracite coal—the very hard, black coal—was created.

When humans discovered that this black rock could be burned to provide energy, coal mining flourished. Harry's son, young and not yet seeing the bigger picture, once questioned why his father had to participate in such a "brutish, savage occupation" that seemed to him to pillage from the earth's ground. To dig through the earth's crust, altering the beauty at the surface in the process, was troubling to him. He argued that "We should be pushing harder for green energy! Now, Dad, wouldn't it be nice if I could travel to places in the world that did not have efficient energy sources and roll in and set up green energy systems to help them out?"

Monday morning arrived and Harry went off to work in the mine a few miles from his home. Arriving at the parking area, he locked his car and checked in at the main building. Today was the day he was to begin excavating a new offshoot tunnel from the main thoroughfare, an act he had been questioning. He knew mining well after working in it for thirty years now. He just felt that the digging of this particular tunnel, despite the coal company taking the numerous standard safety measures, would be jeopardized by the specific layout of the past abutting excavations. He was chided by the management and even by most of his coworkers for being overly cautious. This particular type of tunnel and location was "revolutionary," everyone agreed, and it would yield great returns.

In the end, despite his misgivings about the plan, he submitted to those dominant voices. "I must be getting old," he laughed to himself. "Years ago, I would've never been afraid."

So he adjusted his attitude and proceeded with a renewed confidence. There was coal to be brought to the surface that would help heat people's homes and power industry, all to help humanity. It was a worthwhile and noble undertaking, and he was experienced and qualified to accomplish this. He held a good job and was paid fairly well for his labor, and so he decided not to let his coworkers down.

Harry was part of a ten-man team that would tackle the assignment. Everyone in the group knew each person very well, as they had worked together a long time. Some had twenty-to-thirty years of experience down in the mines. Many of them spent time socializing together outside of work.

They gathered for the upcoming workshift. They dressed with thermal underwear, flannel shirts, blue overalls, rubber steel-toed boots, and sometimes a raincoat and water-repellant pants to help protect from the damp environment they would be subjected to. They wore knee pads. A detachable lantern could be inserted onto their helmets, but could also be attached to their belts.

At last, all preparations having been made, Harry and the rest of the group entered the cart that would lower them down the three-hundred foot slope. The whistle blew and they began the slow descent. It always seemed to take forever to finally arrive at the low point. Once there, they got out of their seats and proceeded to walk five-hundred feet down the straight passageway.

Upon arriving at their destination, they began to excavate perpendicular to the Main Street tunnel, the mine's central thoroughfare. Thus they initiated the new section, which would be nicknamed Tunnel System X. The steel teeth of the continuous miner machine were arranged on an eleven-and-a-half foot-wide cylinder that spun so it could cut and chew into the valuable blocks of anthracite. It would require a few weeks of work to get in far enough to the projected target to be able to extract optimal amounts of the black diamonds. Each team member had specific tasks assigned.

At the end of the workday, Harry showered at the mine site, trying in vain to remove all of the coal dust blackness from his Caucasian skin. Then he went home to his family, where Ann awaited with a hot dinner of meat and potatoes.

Their dining room was in a small space just off the open-concept living room, which had a ten-point buck head mounted on the wall, along with displays of various colorful fishing lures. Harry, like just about everybody else in this Pennsylvania town, was heavily involved in deer hunting and fishing. Ann served venison from the deer Harry bagged last autumn. She kept the meat in individually-wrapped plastic portions in their freezer. She wondered how people could survive back in the old days before refrigeration was invented.

The poor eater of the family was Gregory. Everyone else had finished consuming all the food that was served except for Gregory, who was picking at the remaining morsels, a miserable expression marring his countenance. Some of the food he tried to hide from his parents by stuffing it under the edge of his plate. Another, larger, piece of meat he managed to smuggle down to rest upon one of the cross-rungs of his chair, completely out of sight from the other diners.

Ann, irate with his procrastination, scolded him, saying "Come on, Gregory. The rest of us are counting on you. We get no dessert until everyone is done eating all his food." The boy was about ready to cry, but reluctantly forced himself to ingest another segment of meat.

"Come on, finish it all," said his dad. Well it was to take another ten minutes before Gregory finally completed this hated task and everyone was able to proceed to an ice cream cone.

Harry and Ann went outside, where it was warm. Harry begged her to play her guitar and sing for him. She ran downstairs to the basement and brought the instrument outside to the porch where she began to softly sing *Tecumseh Valley*. She had a beautiful, smooth voice and Harry remained fixated on her blue sparkling eyes, which closed a while, then opened to look at him several times during the course of the song.

There was a pleasant surprise that made both of them smile: toward the end of the song, a saxophone began playing along from elsewhere inside the house. It was their son Mark who was in his room improvising while he played along with his mother. He was very talented and could usually hit the right notes. His improvisation sounded great and he only squeaked two notes. When the song was over, Harry and Ann clapped for the unexpected musical accompanist!

After dark, the family gathered in the backyard to gaze up at the stars. "Amazing how they just stay up there and shine," said second-grader Gregory.

"They look so close . . ." added Ann.

"But they're very far away, Mom! Light years away! It would take a long, long time to get to one of them—if you had a spaceship that could get you there!" answered Mark, a fourth-grade honor roll student.

At the end of the evening, everyone went to bed. "Good night, Mom! Good night, Dad!" Lights went out.

After several weeks were spent excavating Tunnel System X, one day Harry held up his lantern and smiled upon unveiling a fortuitous discovery. The vein was indeed richer in coal deposits than any other he had seen before. He cried out, "Yes! Good deal!" and could not wait to report his findings to his crew and the people at the ground surface. He began striding triumphantly toward the main thoroughfare of the mine where the rest of his crew and the miners from other teams working different shifts were taking in a half-hour break.

He whistled and smiled to himself as he made his way to Main Street. Suddenly, without warning, the ceiling and walls collapsed about three-hundred feet from where Tunnel System X intersected with Main Street. Rubble filled that section, effectively trapping him in the narrow passageway, separating him from his work team and the rest of the miners.

A large block of rock fell on his leg, twisting it severely. He was unsure if any bones were broken. His immediate problem was to extricate himself from under the rock. With all his force, he attempted a few times to lift and push it away but was thwarted by its superior weight. Dust filled the air, making him cough. He felt debris get into his eyes, making it a difficult task just to try to see what was going on.

He rested a minute and then tried again to lift the rock and this time just barely succeeded in freeing his leg, but in the process felt a painful tear of his lower back muscles. That made him nauseous and light-headed, and he could not immediately get up from the dirt floor. But at least he was free of being pinned down.

He felt water rushing over his boots. The mine was flooding. He figured they had cut away too much coal, compromising a thin section of rock wall so that a previously-mined tunnel that had long ago filled with groundwater now had been exposed. According to the maps used for planning their strategy, that wall was supposed to be hundreds of feet thick. If he was correct in his surmise, there could be one-hundred fifty million gallons of water in the old abandoned mine compartments that now sought to relocate to the current site of active operations.

A sickly feeling beheld him as he lay there. "What have I gotten myself into?" he thought. With much difficulty he managed to raise himself from the ground. He attempted to walk and at first felt stiff with pain. After he took a few steps, the agony lessened a little, enough for him to move about more, although with a degree of painstaking effort.

All he could hear was the raucous rush of high-pressure water into the tunnel, which had created so strong a current that he had a difficult time struggling to avoid getting knocked down and carried away with the raging subterranean river. The water level was rising fast. Already it was up to his knees.

He could not get out of the tunnel because of the massive amount of debris blocking the exit. He could tell the water was also flooding the other side of this barrier. Neither Harry nor anyone on the opposite side of the cave-in could dig through the rubble successfully in time before the water would fill this low-lying area. In the initial moments following the collapse, he could hear the men shouting frantically back and forth but could not discern exactly what they were saying because the sound was greatly muffled. At least on their side there was access to the inclined plane exit ramp on which they could ride or walk out to safety. Normally, it was a half-hour long ride out. He prayed that the rest of his friends could outrun the rising water and make it successfully to that place of egress.

Unfortunately, on this side of the blocked tunnel, the only hope he had for himself was to attempt to outrun the rising water as he hobbled on his injured leg to get to as high a ground as could be found in the tunnel system. He knew there were a couple places that might meet those favorable specifications.

The tunnel was only four to four-and-a-half feet high. He stood over six feet tall, and so had to continually bend over as he maneuvered through the tunnel away from the water leak. He had only the light from his headlamp to guide him. In pain, he pushed himself as hard and as fast as he could in traversing through the passageways.

He tried to outrun the deluge but before long, the water was up to his chin, his head bumping into the coal ceiling as he struggled to keep his mouth and nose above the water, which was frigid at fifty-five degrees Fahrenheit, and foul-smelling. He was two-hundred fifty feet below the surface of Earth, roughly equivalent to being on the top floor of a twenty-five-story building inverted into the ground. The passageways were only twenty feet wide throughout the maze of this mine, which was arranged like a honeycomb.

Suddenly his heart sank when his helmet lamp illuminated the air ahead just enough so he could see the water had risen all the way up to the ceiling about one-hundred feet in front of him where the path curved down to a lower elevation. He had to turn back and take a right or left at the intersection he had passed a little while ago. He turned around and proceeded back to from where he just came. When he came upon that interchange in the road, he took a left and, in time arrived at a corridor where the water was only as deep as his feet.

While he was struggling to survive, the rest of the miners scrambled to do the same. Initially they tried to dig out the rubble to get to Harry, but had to abort that because of the rapid flood that overtook them in the first few minutes. Initially they tried to ride the conveyor cart up, but the flooding water knocked out all the electric power, and so they had to abandon that idea. On foot, they discovered one exit blocked by a wall of four-foot high water which effectively occluded that passageway. The only other exit had a swift, cold current raging with so much force that it greeted them by knocking them down as if they were bowling pins. The water, about twenty feet across, was two feet deep, but for men crouching in a four-foot high passageway this meant the water was up to their chests. They had no choice but to get across the turbulent torrent. They managed to cross into higher ground and then proceeded to hike as fast as they could. About fifteen to twenty minutes later, they were finally free of the water. It took another half-hour or so to walk the rest of the way to the portal of the mine, where they were greeted by workers at the surface.

Meanwhile, emergency workers congregated on the grounds above the mine. Because the mine was flooded, there was no chance of sending workers down to try to dig out the obstruction where the roof had collapsed. They had to hope Harry would make his way to a high point, ahead of the rising water. And they had to get as many pumps as they could into the subterranean maze and pull that water out as fast as possible. They spread out maps of the mine showing the layout of all the passages. They used global positioning satellite technology to determine where they should drill down to pierce into some central part of the mine shaft so they could then try to install an air pipe.

They settled on a patch of ground on a dairy farm just off the highway. The farm owners welcomed the rescue crews, opening their home and barns to them, providing a base of operation where the workers could use the bathroom, get snacks, wash up, and stay abreast of all developments in the rescue effort. The farmer's property would indeed be messed up very much because of the muddy footwear and dirty clothing of the rescuers, and his family's previously quiet and private life would be severely disrupted, but the farmer and his family could care less; they just tried to be as helpful as everyone else at this desperate time.

Requests were disseminated asking anyone with pumps to help out. Many volunteers came forward and began drilling bore holes, into which lines were then worked down so pumps could pull the water out of the mine shaft.

In addition to the smaller holes dug to siphon water, a larger, six-inch diameter hole needed to be drilled so an air tube could be inserted to blow hot oxygenated air down into the ground. Not only would this help to warm the chilled air of the mine but it was hoped it would repel the rising water when its pressure exceeded that of the surging liquid. It could take about two hours to drill this through two-hundred fifty feet of solid rock.

While all this activity went on at the ground surface, Harry kept up his fight to survive. Once again, the water rose to his chin. He had to keep his head tilted to the side to keep his nose and mouth above water while his head banged and scraped against the rough, irregular ceiling of coal and other rocks.

After a while, he was able to arrive at a place where the water was not yet so high. As he continued making his way along this passage, the water level got lower and lower, until eventually his feet were on dry ground. He followed an abrupt turn in the path and continued down this passageway. He went as far as he could, perhaps another thousand feet, until he realized he had come to a dead-end. Now he really was trapped. There were no more choices. This passageway was his final alley where he would make his last stand. He believed he was at the farthest reaches of the mine, about a mile-and-a-half from the exit. But, he surmised, this was the place down here that was at the highest elevation and so offered him at least a slightly improved chance that he might survive if the water level would just peak short of where he now waited.

He turned around and returned to where the water levels were only an inch high. There he discovered cement blocks that were stacked and stored along the edge of the tunnel. He began manipulating them, frantically erecting a wall that could possibly serve as a dam. But he soon found it to be difficult to breathe. The air had so little oxygen in it. It was the black damp that miners feared. He vomited. He was able to put up only a smidgen of what would be required of the dike when he realized the water level was rising faster again and had penetrated onto the cement blocks. His energy and spirits were drained and he felt very ill.

He moved away from the cement blocks, navigating through the abrupt turn in the path. To conserve the battery in his lamp, he extinguished it. All was quiet. The darkness was so black he could not see his hand in front of his face. Besides hearing drops of water dripping occasionally from the roof, all else remained tranquil and silent.

Eventually he felt a little better. He collected his thoughts and tried to reassess his situation. He was entombed deep inside the earth. He had no way of knowing how bad the collapse had been and to what extent. He only hoped the workers at the surface could guess his location and somehow get him out in time. At least he was still able to hobble around on the injured leg. He sat on a chunk of coal. The water was now only rising slowly, much slower than before, and he was grateful for that.

He ate a half of the corned beef sandwich he had in his back pouch, the only food that was available. It was enclosed within a plastic Ziploc bag and so remained dry despite the fact that his clothes were entirely soaked. He was famished and thirsty but at least had this. He saved the other half for later.

He turned his lamp on and saw a small brown rat looking at him. He could discern the petite oval ears, the snout, and the thin whiskers in the dim light. He marveled at the creature's tiny fingers and hands. It just sat there about two yards away. They stared at each other a long while, studying each other's physical features.

"Are you alone?" Harry asked. It continued looking at him for another minute before scurrying away into the black nothingness.

Suddenly, he heard machine-like rumblings vibrating through the ground from afar. This went on for a few hours, gradually ascending in volume like a beautiful crescendo until reaching a dynamic climax when suddenly a six-inch drill penetrated the ceiling about twenty feet away from the place where he waged his incomplete attempt at a dam. Miraculously, the workers at the surface had guessed correctly as to where he could most likely be! It took a long while, but the drill was eventually completely withdrawn. Then an air pipe was inserted and maneuvered down into position.

At the surface, Ann Smirkowsky waited in desperation along with the other spouses and family members of the miners who had escaped. She brought the three boys with her and they joined up with other kids their age. When the drill broke through, a strong blast of "bad air" containing low levels of oxygen was received. Rescue workers looked worriedly at each other upon sensing, correctly, the poor quality air, fearing the miner would have trouble breathing. Word travelled around and eventually Ann and her kids received the unsettling news.

But then the rescue workers signaled that they could detect a banging on the air pipe. Harry had begun repeatedly tapping on the pipe, using a rock, hoping it would be heard all the way at the surface. Now the rescue team knew he was alive. The workers hit the pipe repeatedly, and were answered with a ping from below each time. Harry continued to bang on the pipe until he was convinced he heard pings of acknowledgement arrive from the surface. He now was sure that they knew he was alive! Ann gasped in relief, at least for now, as she continued to pray like never before.

As soon as possible, the workers began pumping compressed air into the pipe with the hope that it would push back against the water to stop it from rising any further. They had to figure out how many pounds per square inch of pressure would be required to accomplish that. They cranked up the rig's air compressor as high as possible since they were aware they could not form a completely impermeable seal at the surface and so some air pressure would be wasted. Volunteer firefighters packed dense bags, normally used to lift wrecked vehicles off crash victims, around the hole where the air pipe entered the ground to try to limit the amounts of pressure lost. Also, the air was heated to one-hundred ninety degrees in hopes of warming the air around Harry, which was probably about fifty degrees.

Then the heated, compressed air roared down. The rate of pressure was so great that it was extremely loud, so much so that it caused pain in Harry's ears and he found himself cupping his hands over them to gain some degree of relief.

Having left his wristwatch back at the check-in station, he had no idea that twenty-four hours had now elapsed since he entered this circus.

Despite the efforts of the drill team, the foul-smelling orange-colored water continued to rise and, after many more hours transpired, eventually inundated the passageway around the air pipe so that the trapped miner could no longer reach it to bang on it. He had to retreat farther up the dead-end road. The water was moving a little faster now, progressing gradually toward him, a few inches at a time. He huddled against the wall at the end of the tunnel and felt his time on Earth was coming to an end. How he had managed even to get this far remaining alive amazed him.

Into the second day of being trapped, the pain from his leg injury worsened. He knew it had swollen a great deal. Despite the hot air being blown in, it was still cold and damp down there, albeit better than what it had been. And it became so quiet, the noise from the air tube having diminished substantially now that he was farther away from it, and because the tip of the tube was close to being submerged. He yelled a few times, foolishly hoping someone at the surface might hear. He figured they must have run into problems since there was no more activity indicating progress in getting a rescue device to him.

Then time further elapsed and he got swallowed up into the placid stillness as the dust continued to settle from the turbulent incident that happened now more than forty-eight hours ago.

Harry wondered if he had lived a good life. Faced with his imminent death, he began thinking about the time he had given two bucks to a homeless man despite his friends scoffing at him for doing so. "You're just throwing money away foolishly," they said. He thought about it and agreed with them. "Yeah, probably am." But then he gazed again into the weathered face of the man with the dull, vacant eyes and just saw someone who was really down and out for reasons he could never really know. "Maybe one day that could be me," he thought, as he reached out to present the money to the grateful human being.

He wished someone could reach him now, down in this black hole in the earth, wished someone would give him a handout of some sort to lift him out of this predicament. "Please, is anyone up there? Talk to me! Can you get to me?" he cried aloud, his voice finally trailing off in weakness. He started to believe that, despite the people at the surface having found his location, malfunctions were being encountered in the attempt to rescue him. He knew how these things went down—always defects, shortcomings, and unexpected delays and obstacles to overcome.

He had been staring into the darkness for so long now that he actually began to believe he could discern his boots in the pitch blackness. He shook his head as if to wake up from a dream, but then thought he could see a sky with twinkling stars shining down upon him. He imagined the Big Dipper hanging in the benighted air to his left, the Little Dipper to the right. One time, he thought he saw a little town with houses and trees. Of course he knew he could not actually be seeing these things. He thought he was going crazy and so he switched on his lantern. Its light intensity had become dimmer as the power source gradually was drained. But at least he could see around him. With the light on, he saw no constellations or villages—just black coal.

The captive inside the rocks of the earth mused, "How was I supposed to have lived? I know I sometimes drank and smoked too much. And cussed. I treated some people badly at times. I lied and cheated on occasion. I'm sorry for that! I am! For all those things! I really am sorry! I'm so sorry for everything! But I never killed anyone. Didn't do that, unless you include what I did in that damned Vietnam place. No, that don't count. 'Cause they said to do it, that it was for a rightful cause. It don't count."

Harry held his head by his hands. He felt the moisture from his eyes escape to roll down into the valleys of his face. He prayed like his church taught him. He resigned to the approaching fact that he was going to "meet his maker," like his dad used to say in jest. This, however, was no joke now. But Harry laughed to himself anyway. Then he wept aloud and yelled so that another person trapped in a far corner of the mine, if that were the case, would have heard him.

He began to realize all that he would miss with Ann and the kids and his friends. He started wishing he had done things differently.

He wanted to hang in there for as long as possible. He was determined to budget his half-sandwich, so he planned to eat only a portion of it at this time. He took a nibble. He drank water from an unopened bottle he found.

Then, looking up, he noticed the rat had returned. Breaking off a small piece of the sandwich, he very slowly, without any jerky movements, stretched out his arm so the smidgen of food held between his fingers was brought closer toward the little animal. He moved so slowly, perhaps over the course of as much as fifteen minutes, because he did not want to scare it away. The rat did not run away.

At last, when the food was an inch away from the rat's mouth, it stretched itself so it could eat the portion out of his hand. After the curious rodent finished, Harry ate the remainder of his own portion.

"What are we going to do?" Harry asked, chuckling that he was trying to communicate with a rat. "We lived our best, didn't we? We tried, right?" The animal remained there awhile, staring at him, but then disappeared somewhere beyond the range of the dimming, now flickering, light.

As minutes turned into more and more hours, the water level crept toward him so that he was forced to retreat to the final patch of dry ground, which was only a twenty-by-thirty feet area against the dead-end tunnel walls, which were rough-hewn and irregular with various holes and coves breaking up the surface plane.

It was then that he stumbled into a partial awareness of that oneness. It took this calamity to block his vision of his actual surroundings but simultaneously pry open his eyes to this something else. Forced into a confined position with no way out on his own, facing imminent death, he suddenly came to see that everything was unmistakably one thing.

Strange now for this to happen. He laughed, "Was I too busy to slow down to see it before? Was I that closed-minded? How did I miss the boat? Then again, I really don't think I know anybody close to me who was anywhere near getting on that boat. It was just foreign to all of us. I guess there are people who do see it—but I don't think too many."

With this new possession clear in his mind, he acknowledged that he now wished he had it long ago because perhaps there would have been so, so much, more he could have done for the sake of the world, for everyone else. "Why didn't I think of this?" he muttered. He began imagining a kind of universal love and respect that his kids and their friends would embrace.

Meanwhile, as Harry sat on a boulder of coal and waited, and waited, there had been much activity at the ground surface. A super bit had arrived, still unassembled, escorted by police vehicles blaring sirens. This drill began chewing a thirty-inch hole through the ground to create a rescue exit. The workers at the surface had guessed, if everything went right, that this could reach the mine seven or eight hours later. Then it would take an additional three or four hours to retrieve the drill and lower a rescue basket down. But they would find that things were not to go as smoothly as they hoped. Harry was correct when he figured there were problems.

The rescue coordinators were gravely concerned that if the pressure was to drop too suddenly once the super bit punched through, Harry could be subjected to the bends, a condition in which bubbles could fatally form in the bloodstream. Naval experts were dispatched to the scene along with a hyperbaric chamber that could be used if he experienced any signs of the bends.

Ministers provided counseling to the family members. The Ladies' Auxiliary brewed coffee for the people assisting with the rescue effort. Ann needed to do something to keep her mind stable amidst the unnerving waiting and chaos. She helped prepare and pour the coffee. Portable toilets had been trucked in. Financial donations poured in. Food was donated including pizza, sandwiches, and rigatoni with meatballs.

Everything was bumping along at the surface until suddenly everything stopped abruptly—the super bit broke at one-hundred five feet into the ground. It had to be teased back out before drilling could resume, not an easy task. They estimated it could take a week to do that.

Ann dejectedly left the rescue site to sleep at home for the night. On the way there, they encountered the fire company's annual picnic. A few people danced to the polkas played by a local band, the Pennsylvania Merrymakers. Ann had pierogi and potato pancakes, as did the kids. Gregory was suddenly a voracious eater.

Back at the rescue site, everyone continued working feverishly to try to retrieve the bit. Meanwhile, a second hole would have to be cut about seventy-five feet away from the first. This drill, however, was destined to fracture as well.

A special tool was improvised by a local shop. It was hooked up and sent down the first hole where it met up with the severed drill bit. The workers got it to grab a hold of the 1,500-pound broken part, and gradually tugged, twisted, and manipulated it up out of the hole. After fourteen hours had elapsed since the bit broke, now a new one could go back to work.

At the end of the third day, Harry again heard tapping from above. They had to be coming to save him, he hoped. He ate the remaining food and lapped water from a rocky ledge. And at last the water level ceased its advance.

But then he waited yet another day. At least when he turned on his light to check the water level, he saw clearly that the water had actually been receding greatly and this gave him more hope. Then he heard digging noises again getting closer. At last the drill cutting a rescue tube passageway poked through the roof of what he thought would be his own tomb. They had reached him.

He was hungry and weak. He waited patiently. He tried to think positive thoughts. The drill bit backed out and then a rescue tube appeared after yet another eternity of waiting. A rescuer emerged and greeted him.

He was helped into the tube by the brave man, secured, and then made the long journey up through the ground to finally emerge at the surface, nearly eighty hours after having been trapped in this bad hair day. The drill shaft had pierced through an aquifer and so Harry had to face a barrage of cold water infiltrating the rescue capsule on the way out, like the earth wanted to rub salt in his wounds just before he was to escape its ferocious grip.

When he stepped out of the vessel, his face black with coal dust, he asked for a minute to himself, during which he took a few steps toward the edge of the woods, hobbling on his sore leg. Opening a zipper on his coat pocket, he reached in with his battered hand to carry out a furry creature, releasing him to the woods.

"Live, friend," he whispered, watching it scurry out of sight.

A reporter spoke to his television audience, "In our constant struggle to survive in this world, sometimes we win, sometimes we lose. Looks like this miner will be okay! What a happy day for us all!"

One of the rescuers hustled over to Harry and helped him onto a stretcher, where medics tended to him. Ann ran to greet him. She hugged and comforted him. "I just want to be home with you and the kids. That's all I want," Harry pleaded deliriously.

"You are home," she responded. "And you will always be," she tearfully reassured him.

SIX

I have set pieces of everything on the harsh, rugged, ever-changing ground in front of you, a pair of shoes loosely laced, the ribbons having been gently guided through alternating eyelets, the unfinished ends trailing off to the sides, lying quietly against the trembling floor. But now, after maneuvering so far a distance across vast spans of time in huge corridors of gaseous, dusty space, I take the tips into my fingers, pull tightly and tie them together, securing them to create a strong, cohesive entirety.

Some time ago, my dear cat used up all of her nine lives. She had been a wonderful companion, and I deeply missed her purr, the signal that reassured me she was happy and content.

My own set of lives, if that is what it is, will end soon, too. I was suddenly and unexpectedly overtaken by a series of grave misfortunes and forced to lay low. I had at last become tired and ill from my journey and began to feel myself rapidly approaching an expiration date of sorts. I had become smaller so that I could no longer hope to remain viable. In addition, the space vehicle had worn out to a critical level. Duct tape and a kick here and there could hold up for only so long. I had certainly gotten myself into a dark alley, dead-end jam in this beautiful, cruel world. I would vanish soon, to return finally to stardust.

It had always been my deepest desire to leave behind, to someone who cared, the records of my time watching the construction from scratch of this rocky house and the countless lives that would in turn occupy it. The thought was that perhaps some degree of utility could be derived from it, to be shared by many throughout the world. In the end, I wished my gift would inspire and put all into a meaningful, practical perspective. That's all it was—no more, no less, and I thought it to be a good wish. But I also knew humans first needed to be allowed to work through certain things on their own until an appropriate time would arrive at which my story could then be effective for them. I was aware it would be fruitless to share it before this moment.

I determined that that time had arrived. I felt an urgency in relaying this information now because I detected certain distressing trends where more and more of us were, let's just say, becoming aloof from roots—we were spending too much time inside our cars and plush living rooms, away from the world outside. That was the way I would come to see it.

So I needed a plan to actually get the information to someone. The question was just how to send out this message-in-a-bottle so it could actually be found. This meant so much to me that, despite my sorry state of affairs I made the decision to get my memoir and film to people at a place I most trusted. They were on the other side of the world, a mere brief moment of travel in years past but no longer the case due to the poor condition of my formerly reliably vigorous space car. I embarked on this risky journey which took a long time as I pushed to maneuver through violent storms and turbulence in terrible conditions. It was a bumpy ride interrupted frequently by mechanical failures. I found myself on numerous occasions banging on the engine with all kinds of tools, urging the vehicle onward, shouting "Come on! Get going! Come on, do once more what you did so many times for me!" It took a great effort.

When at last I arrived at the destination, I set up my story on an uncontaminated microscope slide and created a series of explosions full of smoke and glittery particles that would attract attention. The details of this spectacle are unimportant at this time. When the documents were actually seen and the man and the woman recognized its value, and they began spreading the word of a notable discovery, and the experts plunged themselves into a sustained analysis of it that could not be turned back, I at last was able to smile as I laid back and breathed a calmness that I had indeed accomplished my mission, despite so often feeling I'd fall short. Koobi and his family would have found peace, now knowing unequivocally that Punga, even in death, was home. And Otabu would have smiled.

But it took its toll. I was banged up and bruised, and my eyelids were heavy. My feet fell asleep and my nose was congested. Laughing, I wrapped cartoon-character Sponge Man bandages around my bloody forearm and leg. I moved sluggishly. It was a long expedition that finally took its toll on me. With deepest sorrow, I say goodbye now.

The road was more than I originally conceived. The road was a universal idea built up from and linking all that ever existed. Even though I was far away from the place where I was born and could never get back there, I became quite aware of how that did not really matter, because I was as much a part of your planet as you mine. We were on the same road, along with all the animals and plants and rocks. I was actually home, after all. We were all home, in the great oneness of it all, and always would be. The universe was me, and you, and everything and everybody else. All one, all home.